Altered

D.L. Gardner

D. L. Gardner
Copyright © 2016 D. L. Gardner

ISBN 13 – 9781386600688

Information may be obtained by contacting
9385 Olalla Valley Rd SE Port Orchard WA 98367

Altered
*is dedicated first to my grandchildren and great
grandchildren, whom I hope will have the opportunity
to live in and enjoy the beauty of a clean and thriving
world.*

*Secondly, I dedicate this book to all the organic farmers
throughout the world. Thank you for thinking of the
future!*

Privatol

The door slammed open against the wall, and a gust of summer air heated the living room. Nathan tossed the newspaper on the couch and rose in time to catch the brass knob before it made a hole in the sheetrock. The stopper had already been broken from his sister's last fit.

"What the heck, Abree?" He glared at the freckled-faced twelve-year-old standing on the porch.

A wadded ball of green paper hit him on the chest and fell at his feet. "I'm not going!" His sister's hazel eyes locked onto his, her cheeks a brilliant pink.

"Not going where?" Nathan stooped to retrieve Abree's projectile and unfolded it. He already knew where. Ivana had sent him a message earlier in the afternoon alerting him to the alleged National Emergency, and the government's campaign to send elementary school children away. To where? No one knew. Maybe Abree's note would say. As he read, reality pierced his heart. The Grays were going to take her. Abree's reaction was no surprise.

"You know where," she said. Her lips curled into a sneer as she pushed past him and fell onto the couch. She was braver than most girls her age. She didn't cry. It wasn't her nature. But the way she looked at him he could tell she was angry. And fearful.

"You're just a kid, Bree. You have to do what they tell you to. I wish it weren't that way, but it is."

"Do you do what they tell you?" She squinted at him.

Nathan didn't answer. His disdain for the men in the gray uniforms was nothing he wanted to feed his little sister. She had enough of her own resilience.

"See?" You don't. Well, I'm not leaving Mom." Abree jumped up again, bumping her knee on the coffee table as she did. Her face flushed as she rubbed the impending bruise. "What will the Privatol do to me if I don't go?"

It couldn't be good. The Grays were ruthless and intimidating. Nathan had watched the soldiers arrest his friend Roger Frankfurt the week before. No one had seen or heard from the teenager since, not even Nathan's mom who was best friends with Roger's parents. Nathan never told Abree about Roger. Why scare her?

"Just do what you're told and spare us the consequences." Nathan pulled his phone from his pocket and thumbed a text to Ivana, asking how her twin siblings, Carlos and Maria, were handling the news.

"Yeah right, do what I'm told!" Abree made a face and put her hands on her hips. "Go to boarding school like a nice little girl. Whatever! Singing songs, so happy!" She skipped around the house chanting, her act a trifle too melodramatic for Nathan to conceal his smile. "Oh yes, we want to leave our mommies and our comfy bedrooms, and our bikes and skateboards and our brothers. I just can't wait!"

"Abree!" Nathan shook his head. "Stop that."

"Well? Isn't that what they expect? For us to be all cheery and excited to go with them?"

"Apparently not. That's why they're calling in the National Guard!" He nodded toward the newspaper he'd been reading. Terror filled her eyes and Nathan immediately regretted telling her about the added militia being summons. "I'm sorry, Bree. I didn't mean to scare you."

"I didn't know they were calling the National Guard? Are they going to kill us?"

"They better not. I'll...." Playing along with her antics, he punched his fist into his hand and set his jaw. "I'll slaughter every last one of them one by one. I'll rip their heads off!" He contorted his face and grabbed the imaginary enemy by the neck, twisting his arms as if decapitating a body.

Abree laughed. "You look funny when you do that."

Nathan smiled; glad he made her laugh, and glad he got her mind off the fact that within twenty-four hours she might be leaving home and living somewhere else. Neither he nor his mother would know where. He boiled inside and her laughter kept him from thrusting his fist through the wall. If he could kidnap her and Mom and hide away somewhere, he'd waste no time. But for all the plotting and scheming he did these last two weeks, the Gray's were always one step ahead of him.

Abree's frown returned. "They might. Kill us, I mean."

"No one's going to hurt you, Bree. Why would they hurt a bunch of children? Maybe they're just going to test you, like they've been testing me and Vana and the other kids in my class."

"What kind of tests?"

Nathan shrugged and picked up the paper, rolled it into a tube and bopped her on the head. "Easy tests. You're smart. You'll ace them."

"I don't do well with tests. I hate tests." She tried grabbing the paper from him but he held it over her head.

She shouldn't read the news. Not now. Not ever. Why can't she just stay innocent and not be a part of this mess? "The Grays don't grade the tests. They're more like the aptitude tests we used to take. Remember those? To see how smart you are and what kind of skills you're good at? My civics class gets them every day now."

"Every day?"

"Yep. At least one test a day, each one on a different subject. We had a test today that was about farming. Get this. They wanted to know what I knew about raising corn! I didn't do well. I know nothing about farming, really."

"You should. I do."

Nathan chuckled but his smiled faded when he saw how serious she was. "What do you know about farming?"

"All there is to know. You put a seed in the ground, you water the seed, and it grows into a plant, which makes more seeds and then the cycle starts all over again. We learned that in kindergarten."

"This test was a little more complicated then basic horticulture. Most of the questions were about genetic engineering, insecticides, pruning, and things like that. I was totally lost."

"Oh. I don't know about that either. Did you fail?"

He shrugged. "I don't know. I think I might've got some answers right."

"Why would they ask you about farming? There aren't any farms around here. That's dumb." Abree bounced back on the couch and grabbed the remote from the coffee table. She clicked her way through the menus on the screen and loaded a video game. "Still I'm not going to a boarding school. Even if they did put this dumb bracelet on me."

"Bracelet? What bracelet?"

Abree rolled up her sleeve and thrust her arm in the air. Wrapped around her wrist was a metallic black band with a tiny row of lights blinking on and off. Nathan fell on the couch next to her and took her arm. "This is more than just a bracelet! What is it?"

"A tracer. They put one on every student at school, even the recess monitors."

Nathan took a deep breath when his eyes met hers. Holding back his wrath wasn't easy but he mustn't let Abree see his rage. Doing so would only feed her defiance. And then what would happen? "Not good!" Nathan maneuvered the band around her wrist looking for a clasp. The instrument had an ominous final feel to it, like a brand on steer before slaughter. "I don't like this at all!"

"It's okay. We just have to wear it until we get on the bus tomorrow. They promised to take it off then."

Nathan's eyes widened. The bus? Tomorrow?

Abree's eyes narrowed. "Except I'm not going to be on the bus tomorrow. They'll have to go without me."

The hum of the garage door interrupted them. "Mom's home. She'll know what to do!" He tried to sound reassuring but with his own anger stirring, it wasn't easy. "Maybe you'll be away for only a couple of weeks or something."

The kitchen door slammed shut and the sound of high heels on linoleum announced their mother's arrival. Nathan jumped up from the couch and rushed into the kitchen. Molly Barber was pulling canned goods out of a grocery bag and setting them on the table.

"Mom," he began. "We have a problem. Abree…"

Molly turned to Nathan. Panic paled her face and dried streams of mascara lined her cheeks. Her eyes glowed red. "I don't know what to do," she interrupted.

"About the boarding school?"

Nathan's mom wiped her face with her sleeve and turned her back to Abree standing in the doorway..

"Nathan, please get Bree's suitcase out of the garage."

"Mom!" Nathan protested. "You aren't actually going to let her go, are you?"

"Just do as I say. We need two large suitcases. We'll pack one with supplies and the other with her clothes. They gave us a list. We're to send food. Everyone has to contribute to the boarding school. They wanted just about everything in our cupboards, more, in fact. I had to stop at the store."

"What? You had to buy food for them? With the economy the way it is? That's crazy!"

"Yes, Nathan. I know it's crazy."

"Isn't anyone fighting this? What about the Johnsons? The Hunters? Everyone is just going to let the Grays take their kids away? No one's protesting?"

Molly glanced at Abree and as Nathan moved toward his sister she grabbed his arm; her whisper an angry hiss. "You are not going to cause trouble, do you understand? I'll not have them take both of my children. Now get the suitcases. Go!" She shuffled through the kitchen, pulling boxes of dried food and jars of peanut butter out of the cupboard, stacking them next to the cans.

"No mom, this isn't right. I'll take her place!"

"They don't want you, Nathan. They want the elementary school children. They wouldn't accept the trade and we'd get in trouble for trying."

Nathan hesitated. If he pulled the suitcases out of the garage he'd be giving in to the insanity. He'd be admitting defeat. He paused to catch his breath and control his temper, his words softer. "Why are they making you clear your cupboards, Mom?"

"How should I know?" she mumbled rummaging through the shelves. "They aren't missing a single resource. I stopped at the grocery store and, lo and behold, another supply list. Ralph's is just about sold out!" she sneered. "So efficient, aren't they? So well organized and prepared for any National Emergency that might arise. What a world!"

"Mom?" Nathan eyed his sister's scowl. She was dependent on him to change their mother's mind. He turned his back to his sister, his voice trembled. "We can't send Abree away."

"Abree, go get your bathrobe out of the dryer, please."

Abree remained frozen, staring them. "I'm not going."

"Abree, do what I tell you." Molly demanded. Abree's eyes shot Nathan a plea and it broke his heart. He had no solution for her. She stomped her foot and ran down the hall.

"We can't show her how upset we are, Nate. We can't send her away afraid."

"Why are we sending her away at all?"

"What else are we going to do? The streets are swarming with soldiers. You don't know what's happening out there, Nate! The media is not reporting all of the hysteria. They've brought tanks in. You were in school so you didn't hear, but traffic was held up today because of a protest downtown. People were shot. Kids your age. Killed! Maybe you knew some of them. Maybe they were your friends. I don't know how many were killed or wounded. Worse, the Grays aren't taking prisoners to the jail, Nathan. The protesters are being hauled out of town in swat trucks. Who knows what the soldiers are doing to them?"

Nathan's blood turned ice. This news was far worse than he could imagine. "We can't let them take Abree."

"What do you propose we do? There's no place to hide. No cellars, no attics, no tunnels that they don't know about. They've got helicopters with infra-red lights hovering all over the city. Look at that!" She pointed toward the picture window. Outside a rumble of gray vehicles, a truck and a tank drove by, their motors roaring through the neighborhood as loud as a locomotive's.

"I could get us out of here. Let's just go, Mom--the three of us. We'll sneak away at night. We don't have to stay here."

"Where are we going to go, Nathan? The moon?"

"We could leave the country."

"Where to? Europe? The Privatol owns the world, Nathan. Be thankful for what little we have. At least they aren't rationing the air we breathe. Not yet anyway."

"Mom, there's got to be an escape. This is crazy. You work for a lawyer. Can't you do something?"

"Nathan, no. I can't. No place is safe. The justice system has been overrun. The Privatol has instated their own judges. The lawyer I work for doesn't have much of a voice either. He's lost every one of his cases this month. I wouldn't put my stock in him."

"Then we'll sneak away and hide in the woods behind the golf course. Tonight! We can make a shelter, hunt squirrel. I'm good with a slingshot. They'd never find us. I'll take care of you."

"You're a romantic, son. We wouldn't make it past Oakland Boulevard." Tears ran down her cheeks. She wiped her face, and caught her breath. "You come up with something conceivable and I'll go along with it. I'm just too stressed to even think of an escape. I don't want to see anything happen to my daughter, or my son, but I sure don't know how to prevent it!"

"Fine. Let me think a minute." Nathan paced across the kitchen floor, his mind spinning. "We'll hide in the park above the golf course. I know just the spot. We can leave tonight. It's only an hour's walk."

"They'll find us." Abree had returned to the kitchen, her pink bathrobe bundled in her arms. She stood against the door that led from the kitchen to the garage, blocking the way.

"No, they...." Nathan spun around to argue with his sister, but stopped short when she held up her wrist.

"What's that?" Molly asked and grabbed Abree's wrist. "What is that thing?"

"It's a tracer, Mom. We'll fix this! Right now! With a hacksaw." Nathan reached for the garage door, stopped by his sister's squeal.

"No!" Abree backed away.

"I'll cut it off you."

"No! It sounds an alarm! They warned us at school that if we remove our bracelets a siren goes off in every patrol car out there."

"Who told you that?"

"The Grays! The ones who put the bracelets on us. They'll come shooting. That's what they said!" Tears rolled down Abree's cheeks and she quickly wiped them. "We can't cut the bracelet off because I don't want them to shoot us."

Nathan locked eyes with his mother. Terror paled her face.

"Maybe that's just a scare tactic. Something they told you to keep you from taking the bracelet off," The tremble in her voice told Nathan she didn't believe it.

"I doubt it," Nathan mumbled, reflecting on what his mother told him about the arrests that day.

"It's not worth the chance, is it? What should we do, Abree?" Molly pulled Abree into her arms.

Abree shrugged. "Why do we have to do anything?" She wiggled away from her mother and pouted.

Nathan straightened, wondering if that could work, if they could just stay home and wait the day out tomorrow. Would anyone notice? "What about your tracer?" he asked. "When they come here to find you? Then what?"

"I'll tell them I'm sick?"

Nathan answered her with a snicker. His sister wasn't a liar. She'd never pull a scam like that off.

"If the soldiers were going to look for Abree, they'd come here first." Molly admitted. "I don't think there's much we can do, Nate."

Abree clenched her fist. "If they come here I'll crush them and pull their heads off!"

"Bree don't talk like that." Nathan took her by her shoulders and moved her the few inches he needed to slip into the garage. "Maybe this is only for a couple of weeks. Maybe we're making a bigger deal out of this boarding school thing than what it really is. Maybe it's better to just go along with what they're doing. At least you'll be getting an education."

"I'm not going anywhere!" she screamed, stunning Nathan and Molly into silence. "They can't do this. This is a free country. They can't make me leave my family."

"Abree dear, it's just for a little while, I'm sure. And you can forget about the experience as soon as you get home, I promise. Besides, if you don't go they'll take us to jail and sell our home. Then there'd be nothing left for any of us. And you'd still be taken away." Molly's voice quivered and she bit her lip when she knelt in front of the unyielding freckled-face child. "Look, I don't want you to go either, honey, but doing what we're told right now is the best thing for us. There isn't any other solution."

Abree's fists remained clenched, and her red cheeks swelled.

"Abree," Nathan knelt next to his mother. "If Mom and I can think of a way to get you out of this, we will. I promise you. But whatever we decide to do must be safe so no one gets hurt. Otherwise we're not doing it. Can you understand that?"

He ignored the angry look his mother gave him, no doubt for making a promise he wasn't sure he could keep.

"Your friends will be with you, Bree," Nathan added. His temper was as hot as Abree looked, but his mother and sister needed him to stay cool. He swore to himself he would. For now. He whispered in her ear. "If I could shoot our way to safety I would. I would die for you, Bree."

Abree nodded. Nathan stood.

Molly kissed her daughter's hair. Nathan turned away when he saw tears streaming down his mother's face.

"I know it's tough, honey," Molly whispered. "Let's get some dinner made and pack your bags. You can wear your new jeans tomorrow."

"The ones with the rhinestones on the pockets?"

Before his own feelings gushed out in front of them, Nathan dodged into the garage to get the suitcases.

❖ ❖ ❖

Nathan would have liked to talk to his mother before she went to bed. He hadn't given up on hiding in the woods. If he couldn't persuade her to make a run for it he'd take the chance. Or maybe there was a legal way to keep Abree with them. Maybe they could find a loophole in the law. But Molly hadn't stayed up for him to talk to her. After his mother had tucked Abree in bed, she had slipped into her own bedroom and locked the door.

Nathan couldn't sleep. He paced the floor for a good long while and finally resorted to watching the 10 o'clock news, hoping for more details, but all he heard was the usual propaganda resonating by journalists who'd probably been threatened by the Privatol.

"The children are safer in boarding schools; this action will affect the economy in a positive way." Right! Nathan thought. How stupid do they think we are? Nathan studied the newscaster's face. How could the man spit out lies and remain so calm?

The struggles that single parents have to pay their bills on time will be eliminated."

Nathan snickered. "Of course they will because there won't be any kids to take care of. They won't be parents anymore!"

"The price of food for middle class American families will be more affordable." "Bull! What families?"

"Childcare for working mothers will be of no concern, and everyone will save on gasoline. In addition, the school tax and levies will be eliminated and replaced with one tax for maintaining the boarding school.

Nathan threw the couch pillow at the TV just as his cellphone buzzed. Ivana's text appeared.

"The twins are in hysterics. Mom and Papa are fighting. GTG. Coffee?"

"Be there." He changed the station to the Old Movie channel and turned down the volume before he left. No one ever shut their televisions off completely anymore; the sounds of the city were too terrifying. Sirens, gunshots, police whistles, and dogs barking disturbed the night. He locked the door behind him.

Already past the first curfew, Nathan, being seventeen, was old enough to walk the streets until eleven. Ivana always caked enough makeup on to look like a twenty-year-old, although she wouldn't be seventeen for a few more months.

❖ ❖ ❖

Handy Sam's neon lights shone on the corner of Ash and Pine, a quick walk for both Nathan and the street that Ivana lived on. Inside, three round tables invited the casual patron, but hardly anyone ever used them besides Ivana and Nathan and a few policemen on night shift.

A bell rang when he entered and he nodded to the clerk, an old Chinese man named Jaana. How old, Nathan could never quite decide. The man's face bore a thousand wrinkles, and a small white goatee dotted his chin. His eyes sparkled brightly and he always had a smile for the young people. Nathan pointed to the coffee stand.

"Yes, yes," Jaana said with a smile. "Burritos hot too!"

Nathan chuckled at the thought of Jaana making Mexican food. "No thanks," he said. "Coffee."

Jaana bowed slightly.

Ivana Garcia was at the farthest table watching the door. She smiled when he came in, pulled out her phone and checked for messages. "I can't believe this is happening, Nathan." Her voice was low, but then she barely ever spoke above a whisper when in public places.

"It's repulsive," he agreed, pumping a cup of lukewarm coffee from the carafe on the counter.

"Mom and Papa just about killed each other tonight."

His eyes widened, waiting to see how serious she was. Ivana loved to exaggerate.

"Not really. But yeah, almost—I thought Mom would strangle him. Don't tell anyone I said that just in case he's murdered in the middle of the night."

Nathan glanced around the empty store. "You're kidding, I hope."

"Papa's joining the Grays." She slammed her purse on the table. "He went and got tested and he's been accepted. He's one of them now. He'll take the kids to the buses in the morning and then he's joining their ranks. I can't believe it, Nathan. Mom's a mess. The twins are freaking out. I had to get out of there."

"That's not good news. But then, what is anymore?" Nathan tried to think of some magic words that might comfort her as he pulled up a chair across from her.

Ivana fidgeted with her phone again, pulled a stick of gum from her purse and leaned back against the chair, wiping aside the lone black curl that danced in front of her dark eyes. "How's your mom?" she asked biting into the gum and tossing the curled wrapper on the table.

Nathan shrugged. "Crying behind closed doors. Bree isn't taking it too well either."

"Kid's got spunk. She'll fight them."

"That's what I'm afraid of. What will they do if she does give them trouble?"

It was Ivana's turn to shrug and she did so with one shoulder. "Send her home?"

"You think?"

A siren screamed through the streets as lights flashed into the storefront. The ambulance turned the corner and sped down the boulevard, away from their neighborhood.

"They're still fighting, you know. Nighttime comes and everyone turns into vampires on the warpath, sucking the life out of this city. Sunrise New Mexico is doomed. I wish I could leave. Go back to Mexico and stay with my aunt."

"Is it any better in Mexico?"

"She says it is. She says no one cares what happens in the desert. Cops are scared. I heard you could even have a crop without the bad seed infecting it."

"Did you just say the cops are scared?"

Ivana nodded slightly, her deep brown eyes inspecting his for a brief second.

"Why would the cops be scared?"

"The Cartel and…." She inspected her nails, leaving her sentence hanging.

"And what?"

"I don't know. Something to do with an end-of-the-world. Quetzalcoatl."

"Quetzalcoatl?"

"A dragon," she laughed, "with feathers." She waved the thought away. "It's just a legend. Not my thing."

"How is your aunt getting there? Is that one of the reasons your dad's becoming an Enforcer? Is he taking advantage of the amnesty benefits?"

She shrugged. "I don't know. No one talks. No one tells me anything probably because they know I'll beg to go with them. I'm not ready though.

I'm going to stay and tough it out. Get my degree first before I break my nails with a shovel." She gave him a fake smile. "I'm not a farmer."

If she had asked, Nathan would have agreed. Ivana was a lot of things; strong, spunky, intelligent. But he never saw her get her hands dirty.

Ivana turned serious. "They want us, Nathan."

He leaned back against his chair. The idea of being coveted by the Privatol was not a savory one and sent a fever of dread through his body. "You think?"

"That's why they're testing us."

Nathan straightened and searched her eyes.

Ivana laughed. "Come on, Nate. You don't know?" When he didn't respond, she went on. "They're sizing us up. They want to know how best we can serve them. They have big plans for us. Look, I don't want to scare you or anything, but when they're done with us, we'll all have a slot to drop into. Like a kid's coin bank. They're categorizing us. Filing us away for further use."

"How do you know that?"

"Pfft. *Buen sentido*! Common sense. Can't you see it?"

So involved in their conversation, Nathan failed to hear the bell that Jaana rang. The Chinaman called to them. "Hey! Half hour. Closing shop. Time to go, mon! Curfew."

If Jaana got caught harboring kids their age after curfew he'd face a heavy fine and both Nathan and Ivana would be ticketed. Maybe. After what Mom said about the protesters, maybe the penalty for breaking curfew had worsen. There was no way of knowing. He bounced to his feet. "I can walk you home."

"Forget it. I'll be fine. I'll be at the precinct with Mom and the twins in the morning. Are you going to be there with Bree?"

"I had better." Nathan followed Ivana out the door, handing Jaana a tip as he left.

The Buses

Nathan sat motionless in his mother's SUV in the crowded parking lot the next morning. Like obedient puppets, the whole town had come to deliver their children to the authorities. The scenario sickened him. Most everyone sat in their vehciles, but he could hear the muffled sounds of children crying and an occasional car door slam.

His mom sat in the driver's seat next to him, fidgeting with a tissue. Every few seconds a heavy sigh came from the back seat. He avoided looking at Abree. The pain was too great.

Grays wandered in front of the school. Fully uniformed. Intimidating. Their presence reminded him of his conversation the night before. Nathan chewed on Ivana's words. Why would the Grays want him? He has nothing to offer the Privatol, and if he did, he wouldn't give it to them. Not without a fight.

"I don't know why I have to do this," Abree mumbled.

Molly ignored Abree, wiping her nose. "I don't know where this allergy came from."

The more Nathan thought about what was happening, the angrier he became. He leaned as far back as he could, his arms tucked across his chest, his head hot against the car seat.

Folks were leaving their vehicles, now, gathering in swarms. The local police with their whistles and white gloves kept the pedestrians behind ropes that they had strung across the parking lot.

The National Guard mingled with the parents and children. They were no threat even if they did carry rifles. They lived here. They were friends and neighbors. Nathan recognized a few who had graduated before he did, having attended Central High. They had enlisted only last year, before all this started, wanting to serve their country. They believed in freedom. Freedom. Right!

The Guard's love of freedom is why the other ones are here. The Grays. Nathan chewed the spittle that was forming in his mouth. A slimy ball of disdain. *Filthy pigs!* Stern-faced foreigners who probably can't speak a lick of English. Who knows what language they speak? With machine guns firmly gripped, and rounds of ammunition strapped over their shoulders, they were fearsome. More than fearsome, they were repulsive.

"Who're they planning on gunning down? The police? The guards? The parents? The kids?" Nathan muttered under his breath.

"What?" his mom asked.

"Nothing." He rolled down his window and spat.

The awaited caravan arrived. Long yellow buses. The same school buses that had taken him to school when he was a kid, back in the day when times were peaceful. Before this corporate takeover. Once painted with the school name, the buses now harbored the Gray's seal: a large black circle with a smaller gray one in the center. Nothing more than an elaborate target.

Parents pulled their children out of the way of the rolling cages that seeped their exhaust in puffs of blue smoke. If it hadn't been for the police, no one would have known what to do, but the cops helped everyone into lines as the buses parked.

"Well," Molly sighed. "I guess this is it."

"I'm not going, Mom," Abree said under her breath.

"You're going."

Nathan peered at his mother from the corner of his eye. She was a basket case. Her hair wasn't combed and her eyes were red. She must have cried all night. But she could still punch out that authoritative pitch that made her sound like she meant business. His mother eyed him. She knew that he knew her heart was breaking.

Molly stepped out of the SUV and swung Abree's door open.

"Unfasten your seatbelt, Abree," she said.

"No!"

"Abree," Nathan added.

"I'm not going."

Nathan gritted his teeth, spitting out his anger without turning around. "Look at these men, Bree! They all have guns. Do you have a gun? What will you do if they start shooting at you because you decide to be a little punk? What if they start shooting at everyone because you're acting like a spoiled brat?"

"I'm not a brat."

"Then get out of the car."

Abree groaned. He heard her step out of the car and walk up to his window. He rolled it down.

Their eyes locked. Her cheeks were red, maybe from the cold, maybe not. Her lips barely moved. "I'm scared," she said.

"I know, gremlin. So am I."

"Come with me?"

Mom had already pulled the suitcases out of the back. Nathan slid out of the front seat and stooped next to Abree. He reached in his pocket for his Harley bandana and carefully tied it around her neck. Her eyes grew wide.

"You're giving me your bandana?"

He laughed. "You bet I am."

"I thought that was your greatest treasure."

Nathan forced a smile and touched her freckled nose. "No, Bree. You're my greatest treasure."

He rolled one of her suitcases behind him as they walked. Molly followed with the other. He nodded at his friends when he spotted them, but no one smiled or greeted each other. The crowd was ushered through several different lines, separated by last names and then ushered through another line. A policewoman pointed at Abree, and waved to the direction of her bus. Abree grabbed Nathan's sweaty hand as the crowd shuffled them toward the rumbling vehicles. When they got near the curb, a soldier threw out the end of his rifle, slamming the stock into Nathan's chest.

Nathan jolted from the sudden force. He glared at the man. The Gray's rifle barred him from going farther.

Bree's hand was no longer in his.

"It's just like I said, man." Ivana breathed into his ear as she brushed shoulders with Nathan--the scent of her gum brought him back to reality. Nathan released his fury slowly, silently, though he would rather have punched the soldier in the face.

"Every single person has a slot they'll drop into. Like a kid's coin bank."

Nathan was left with the sickening smell of diesel fuel.

Departure

Abree could barely see through the dirty bus window. Even if she could focus on the landscape whizzing by, tears distorted her vision. Why did Mom make her get out of the car? Why didn't Nathan save her? Why are the Grays bullying her? What's going to happen to her now?

It only took a few minutes for the bus to roll away. Onto the freeway they flew. Exhaust filled the cabin as the driver shifted gears and picked up speed. They merged into traffic, and the little town of Sunrise disappeared behind her, fading into the green and gold of desert.

Would she ever see her home again?

Before she could brood over her misfortune, shouts came from the back of the bus. Abree turned around in time to see Frankie James shake his younger brother violently.

"Shut up, Reggie!" Frankie yelled. "You'll get us all in trouble."

Abree looked around thinking someone should stop them, but there were no teachers aboard and the guard who rode silently by the exit clung to his rifle and stood stiff as a plastic soldier. He had his back to the commotion and didn't even glance over his shoulder.

"Get your hands off me," Reggie insisted. "I hate them. I hate all of them and I'm not going with them."

Frankie laughed and Abree wished he hadn't. She felt just like Reggie did. She wanted to scream just as loud.

"What are you going to do about it, freak?" Brian Gallard leaned into the aisle and sneered at the brothers. He sat across from Abree and had been watching the fight with gloating amusement. Brian was the hall monitor at school. Sixth grade. No one messed with the hall monitors. They were training to be policemen.

"Reggie's brave," Abree whispered under her breath. Brian heard her and swung around sharply. She didn't care what Brian thought. She'd take him on any day of the week. "And honest," she added. "We should all be like Reggie."

"It's stupid to fight the system." Brian barked back. "You won't win. None of us will. You'd best shut up and do whatever these soldiers tell you to."

She squinted at him, his eyes wide and direct, as though her life depended on his wisdom. "I don't have to listen to them. Or to you," she said, her breath chilling as it hissed through her teeth.

"Yeah? Then why are you on this bus?"

She turned with a huff and studied the finger smudges on the window. "Don't talk to me," she mumbled, ignoring Brian's chuckle. Her fingers touched the bandana around her neck as she thought of her brother, her mom and home. An overwhelming pain of loneliness and dread broke her spirit. She dropped her head against the glass and hoped for sleep. She didn't want this. She wanted to be home with her mother.

Jill, a petite, blond-haired girl shuffled into a seat next to her.

"I need to be up front. I get car sick," Jill whispered to Abree, folding her hands on her lap and staring into space through glasses as thick as a fishbowl. "Besides, I don't like sitting next to boys."

"Be my guest," Abree offered without moving, watching traffic whiz by. If she'd been in Mom's SUV with Nate, they'd be counting red cars and slapping each other whenever they saw a Bug. She glanced at Jill and tapped her hand. "Fire bug!" she said, hoping the girl would join in her game.

Instead Jill inched away from her. "Don't."

Abree relented. There was no reason to laugh or play because who knew what was going to happen to them. "Yeah. You're right." Abree rested her head back on the window and closed her eyes, drifting off to sleep.

A sudden bounce over a speed bump woke her. The bus sighed, hissed, and then stopped. Fumes seeped into the cab. Abree sat up straight and watched the sentry jump from the vehicle. The doors closed automatically behind him.

They were in front of a station of some sort. Where, Abree didn't know. She'd never seen this place before. Soldiers roamed the sidewalk guarding a windowless brick building. She counted four National Guard and a platoon of Grays. The sight of the foreign uniforms made her stomach sour, her lips curled in an uncontrollable sneer.

She watched them from her window until her breath made too much steam to see out. She wiped the fog away with her fist.

A sentry met two other soldiers at the rear of their bus and opened the luggage compartment, pulling suitcases out onto the curb. Her red alligator handled suitcase was also pulled from the bus, and the luggage her mom had packed with food.

"Hey!" Abree said as a motorized cart pulled up and soldiers loaded the luggage onto the tram.

Jill leaned over her to peek out the window just as the bus door opened and a woman in a uniform stepped in. She had a clipboard in her hand. Without any introduction, she began reading names like the drill sergeants Abree had seen in movies.

"Jill Newton, Frankie LaMore, Jennifer Crawford, Jim Tennerfore, Robin Bilgrow, Sally McKenzie, Robin Jensen, Andrew McComber, Regimand LaMore, Arthur Hastings," the woman flipped a paper from her clipboard and continued, "Alex Heatherson, Ronald Bearing, and James Rollins, come with me."

When the children that had been named merged from their seats into the aisle, Abree stood also. "Excuse me. You meant to call my name too, didn't you?"

"I don't make mistakes," the woman said without looking at her list.

"But you must have," Abree argued. "Those men outside put my luggage into that cart. So, I think I'm supposed to go with you."

"They took all the luggage," Frankie said as he walked by. He'd been in the back and saw everything.

"That's right. It's no mistake, young lady. You won't be needing your suitcases any longer."

"But what about the food my mom packed?"

The other children grumbled the same question. "Our moms packed food, too!"

The officer snickered bitterly and stepped out of the bus, their questions unanswered.

"Sit down, Abree," Brian said while the others exited the bus. He leaned against the leather seat across from her. Sweat dripped from his forehead. It was hot and stuffy inside the vehicle and Brian was overweight, but he crossed his arms and acted like he was cool.

Abree fell back on her seat and watched through the window as the children swarmed around their guide, a tall lanky soldier with a Grim Reaper face. The sun beat on their heads, their distressed expressions wrenching Abree's heart. She felt sorry for Jill as the frail girl pushed her glasses farther up the bridge of her nose and stood in front of the soldier.

When the woman sentry returned to the bus, the door closed and the engine started up again. Only Abree, Brian, and a dark-haired boy remained. Abree couldn't remember the boy's name, but she had shared a science class with him. A Native American, he was quiet, and smart.

Catching a final glance at the tram with the baggage, Abree gasped. Soldiers were unloading the cargo and tossing it onto a conveyor belt. There went her suitcases with the red faux alligator handles rolling up into a bin, juggling unbalanced with the others before tumbling into a giant compacter.

"Hey!" Abree said and looked at Brian. "Did you see that? All my things were in those bags. And my mom packed a lot of food in the other. They just crushed it all. What gives with that?"

She caught the look of fear in his eyes. They both stared out the window as the bus rumbled onto the highway.

Cells

The hot day passed into twilight and still the bus carried its driver, the three passengers, and the soldier far into a desolate terrain away from Abree's hometown. The sentry took comfort on the front seat near the door. Brian moved to the back to spread out, and the Native American boy was invisible, probably sleeping on a seat somewhere on the bus.

Abree chose to do the same, letting the putrid fumes of diesel, the motion of the vehicle, and boredom lull her to sleep. She woke with a shiver. The sun had taken its final dip into the horizon, and chilly night air seeped through unsealed seams in the bus. Having no coat or sweater to wrap up in, she hugged her shoulders and snuggled closer to the back of the vinyl seats and fell asleep again.

It was late when the engine shut down. The moon was high, though only a sliver and a few stars shimmered against black. Abree stared out the window, wide eyed, and listened to men's voices outside. The door finally opened with a creak.

"Get up," someone ordered. Abree sat upright more from surprise than wanting to obey. "The three of you report to the main office immediately," a man in uniform ordered. His accent was think, his tone coarse.

"Main office?" Abree stood and rubbed her eyes.

"Down the corridor, take a right. The password is written here." The man was so large it was an effort for him to move into the aisle. Instead, he held out a paper printed with instructions and a simple map. Abree blinked the sleep away, attempting to read the words in front of her, but they were in another language. The letters didn't even look like her alphabet.

"I can't read this!" she said as Brian passed by and grabbed the map out of her hands. The Native American boy waved for her to go ahead of him.

The cool of night greeted the three children; a still and lonesome desert sky with infinity twinkling its distant eyes in the heavens. They moved slowly, half asleep—silence so thick it made Abree's ears hurt. The soldier and the bus driver had disappeared into the parking lot, leaving the three children alone in the dark. A few yards away a street-lamp lit the entrance to a building.

"I guess he means down there," Abree suggested.

"Obviously," Brian agreed with a snicker.

Since he had been a hall monitor, Abree trusted that Brian would be able to read the map and navigate, so she followed close at his heels. Through the double doors and down a flight of stairs they passed into a dimly lit hallway. Lamps hung close to the ceiling allowing only minimal lighting. Their footsteps echoed in the hollow tunnel, rattling Abree's nerves. There were no doors anywhere—no office that she could see and nothing that hinted as being an entry or exit. She shivered. "This is spooky!"

Brian stopped. Abree took the map from his hands and turned it upside down, thinking perhaps they'd been reading it wrong from the beginning.

"You had it right the first time," Brian grumbled.

"How do you know?"

"Because that's the way the man handed it to you." He snatched the map back again and flipped it over. "What's your name, kid?" he asked the Native American boy.

"Makia."

"I'm Abree." Abree's attempt to sound cordial failed as her voice trembled and her knees were about ready to buckle. "This dude here is Brian."

The older boy turned to her sharply as though he resented telling Makia his name.

"What?" Abree asked. "We should at least know each other's names. We might as well be friends, since we're in this together."

Before Brian could protest, Makia spoke. "The soldier said to go down the corridor and take a right. There has been no right to take. We might not have gone far enough."

"We've been walking for ten minutes," Abree complained.

"There haven't been any turns. Keep going," Makia insisted.

Abree didn't argue. What good would it do? She didn't have any answers and besides, if they went too far, they could turn around and come back. Perhaps all three of them had the same thought, so they walked on together. However, Abree doubted the decision almost immediately for the hall darkened the farther they went.

"I hope they don't turn the lights out at midnight or something. What time is it now?" Abree asked.

"It's only ten thirty," Makia replied after looking at his cell phone.

"It feels like we're going downhill."

"Yes," Brian answered. "We are."

The walkway narrowed. No longer shiny linoleum walls, Abree realized they were in a natural underground tunnel made of limestone walls.

"I think we've gone too far," Abree stopped—fear seizing her. The others paused and looked around.

"There!" Makia blurted. The three stood fearful for a moment, the cold of the cave chilling their bones. To their right was a large iron door, the most unfriendly entrance Abree had ever seen in her life.

"Welcome to Hades!" Brian snickered.

"That's it," Makia whispered. "That has to be the door the man was talking about."

"I'm not going in there!" Abree cringed. The iron bars and oversized hinges reminded her of doors to castle dungeons she'd seen in fairytale books.

Makia was the bravest. He walked up to the door and knocked, his slender fingers barely making a sound on the hard surface. There was no answer.

"The password. The man gave us a password. What was it?" Makia asked.

Brian unfolded the near torn map and held it as close to the torch above them as he could. "It's foreign."

"Look, though. Those letters are separated. And they're the same on the keypad. Maybe if you just punch them in...."

After inspecting the code, Brian moved past Makia, punched several buttons on the lock and rotated the handle.

Abree gasped when the door opened with a low groan, letting cold air escape from its enclosure into the hall. Fear washed over the boys' faces.

"Well, we're supposed to do as we're told, right?" she asked sneering at Brian. She stepped into the dark, foreboding chamber. Her two companions followed close behind.

A dim ceiling lamp illuminated the empty space. The smell of wet rock and earth filled their lungs.

"I suppose this is the office? Some office! Now what?"

She wished she hadn't asked. As soon as she did, the door sealed shut and the handle rotated into its locked position. A low hum vibrated the chamber, the floor shook, and suddenly Abree had the sensation of falling.

"An elevator!" Staggering, she grasped at the walls.

Unlike the elevators she had been in before, there were no lights signaling the floor number, or controls to stop. Only the horrific feeling of gravity pulling her to the bottom of the earth. Abree and her companions were at the mercy of whoever operated this conveyor, if indeed someone were operating it.

She screamed when the elevator picked up speed. Brian cursed. Makia's eyes opened wide in terror. Abree held her breath, visions of her mom and brother flashing through her mind. *I'm going to die.*

In less than a minute after they had launched, the elevator slowed and stopped. Abree exhaled and focused on the handle of the door, anxious for it to open, yet dreading what might be on the other side. Time hung suspended as they waited. She glanced at her companions, meeting their eyes with mutual alarm.

Finally, the handle turned ever so slowly, and the door gave way to a blast of warm, humid air. A glow of artificial light greeted them. Abree was the first to step out, squinting. The brilliance gave her a headache.

"It's about time you got here," a voice complained.

Abree blinked as the approaching silhouette came into focus. Taller than Brian, yet not much older, a young man in a white smock thumbed through the paper on his clipboard and held out his hand to Brian. "Gallard, I assume?" He tossed his dark wavy hair from his pale skin. His hands were long and slender, almost ghostly. Abree stepped back, glad he wasn't addressing her. "Nam here. I'll be your coach. I've been looking forward to this. Gets lonely down here, but we stay busy."

Brian accepted Nam's handshake. "Where am I?"

Nam laughed, though it was more a cynical laugh than a happy one.

"I can't tell you exactly. Classified information. You'll learn more later," he said. Another skim through his papers before looking up again, he eyed Makia and then glanced at Abree. "You two are in lab."

"Lab?"

"Lab. I didn't stutter. Gallard, come with me. The Labs can wait here."

Brian gave Abree an arrogant grin, clicked his heels he then matched Nam's quick gait, vanishing into the radiance of the hall.

"I wonder what's in store for us," Makia spoke quietly. Though much shorter than she, the boy was Abree's age. She never had a conversation with him at school. He seemed socially withdrawn, and the two had little in common except for their academic abilities. Her peers considered him a brainchild, but among the student body he was a social outcast.

"I wonder what's in store for anyone," Abree said. "You, me, Brian, our families. Who knows what's happening. It isn't good. It can't be."

Makia said nothing, but rather looked around with fearful eyes.

"You two. This way," Nam returned, trotting down the brilliant hallway. He pointed at them and pivoted around. Abree and Makia followed Nam down another long corridor lined with walls of black tile. A long stretch of vacant hallway lay in front of them.

"You, boy," Nam placed his hand on Makia's chest to stop him. "This is your room." He pulled a remote from his pocket and hit a button, triggering a red blinking light on the wall. A panel slid open and revealed a bed encased in a windowless tomb.

"No," Makia said, moving backwards in the direction they had come. Abree thought to join him, but Nam grabbed an instrument which hung from his belt.

"Stop!" Nam shouted. "Run and you'll get more of this."

Makia screamed as his body shook uncontrollably. Abree gasped in horror. Stunned, the boy stood pale and helpless as Nam grabbed his arm and dragged him back.

Nam's eyes caught hers. "Run and you'll be electrocuted," he assured her.

Abree froze, terrified. Her heart thumped wildly.

"Boy, get in your cell. You won't be there forever. It's just for the night so don't get so dramatic. You won't get hurt again if you just do what you're told. They need you."

"Who needs us?" Abree asked.

"Who do you think?" Nam snapped.

"How should I know who you're talking about?"

"Don't play dumb. Both of you kids are here because of your intelligence. The smarter you prove yourself, the better off you'll be. Now get in, I said." Nam pushed Makia into the chamber. Abree watched in terror as the wall slid shut, sealing Makia inside.

"How's he going to breathe?"

Nam didn't answer. "Follow me." He turned his back to her and walked.

Numb from fright, Abree barely felt her legs move as she trailed behind him, wondering how many cells she passed, how many other children were locked up in this catacomb, and whether she'd survive the night.

Nam finally came to a halt and then fumbled in the pocket of his jumper, extracting a handful of small remotes, trying several before Abree's cell opened. He signaled with a roll of his eyes for her to enter, a smug smile on his face.

She squinted at him. "This makes you happy? Electrocuting children? Locking kids up in tombs?" Her heart still thumped in her chest, but fear was quickly turning to anger.

"Yes," he answered. "It's nice to know they're safe and all tucked away for the night. Call it security, if you will. I call it more like isolating ourselves." He gave her a menacing grin. "Something you'll learn more about the longer you're here."

Abree sneered. "You are weird."

"Not really."

"Do they pay you to do this?"

"Actually, quite generously. Now get inside before I do something painful."

Abree felt the heat in her cheeks as she stepped past him. "Don't lose that remote, dude."

"Nam's the name, little girl."

"Yeah? We'll Abree's my name. And don't forget it, or me, or I'll haunt you till the day you die." If she were like other girls her age, she'd be crying right now, but she was too mad to cry. Whoever managed this place had no right to lock her or her friends into a wall.

"Haunt me? Ha! I don't believe in ghosts."

"Well, maybe you should."

Abree stepped inside the room. The door slammed shut. One small lamp built into the ceiling cast enough light to reveal a bed with a foam cushion, and a white jumper that hung on a hook above it. There were no windows, no carpet, nothing that would offer comfort. Only cold black tile walls surrounded her. Abree examined the cell with tears in her eyes and wiped her face with the palm of her hands. "Mommy!" she whimpered, falling prone on the bed.

Thoughts of home swamped her mind. She hated being here. She hated everything that happened today. So immersed in her self-pity she almost missed seeing movement along the dirt floor. She rolled over and blinked. *I'm going crazy.* Her curiosity got the better of her though and she looked again in time to see something wiry disappear into a crack.

Needles

"Come with me." The cell door opened with a startling clang and the image of Nam's lanky body hovered over her. He shone a beam of light around the room. Abree sat upright on the bed, rubbing sleep from her eyes.

"What time is it?"

"Morning. That's all you need to know."

"Morning? It's still dark." She stretched and wiped the sleep from her eyes.

"It's always dark in this wing. Get used to it."

Abree scowled as she yawned, not ready for the day, Nam, or the reality of the miserable world she found herself in the night before. Sizing Nam and his armor, which was nothing more than a taser, a belt with remote buttons, and a stiff white vest wrapped across his chest and back, she snickered. "So, they actually gave you a real weapon? How cool is that? I suppose the vest is so you don't hurt yourself." Her words hid the worry inside. Her stomach growled from hunger, yet she resented Nam's intrusion so much that she refused to tell him she was hungry or scared. "Don't get me wrong. You look cool. Like a Stormtrooper or something evil like that."

He grunted. "My garb is better than anything you'll see in Star Wars. All I need to do to trigger this taser is push this button." He aimed the weapon at the ceiling and touched his belt. White sparkles sizzled into the air. "Now, let's get to work so I don't have to stun you with it. Put that jump suit on."

Abree glanced at what looked like a spacesuit hanging on a hook on the wall. "That?"

"Yeah. Everyone wears them. Keeps your germs from contaminating the air. From now on you'll wear sterile clothing whenever you leave your quarters. You get a clean one every day."

"Maid service? How quaint."

"Enough smartness. Put on that jumper and let's get going. If I'm late I get in trouble and that means you'll be sorry for it."

She glared. "Then you'd better get out of here and give me some privacy."

Nam stepped out.

❖ ❖ ❖

There was only one hall, one dark gloomy path, and only one direction to go once Abree stepped out of the cell. She cringed at the smell, a strong ammonia odor mixed with the mossy fragrance of an underground cave. Though the tunnel was dark Nam's stark white uniform made it easy for her to see him. His stride was much faster than hers and she found herself panting as she raced to catch up.

Nam opened another cell down the hall. A boy dressed in a jumpsuit like hers stepped out. His wide green eyes rested on her for a moment. He brushed his sandy hair behind his ear and smiled.

"Hi. I'm Jaden."

"I'm Abree."

"Get along," Nam interrupted. "This isn't social hour. You'll be testing together."

"Testing?" Abree asked.

"Testing," Jaden whispered in her ear. "That's what they call it but it's more like interrogation. There's a regimen we go through whenever they have a new project for us, to keep a close eye on our intellectual progress," For a boy no older than she was, Jaden's language surprised Abree.

"Who are 'they'?"

"Never mind who they are. That's classified!" Nam barked. "And you'd better keep your mouth shut, O42."

Jaden zippered his lips with a gesture, but gave Abree a nod. She rolled her eyes.

When the three came to a junction, Nam stopped. "You know the process, Lab 042. Inform 067 what she needs to know." He looked over his shoulder, giving Jaden a stern glare. "And only what she needs to know."

Jaden nodded. "Yes, sir."

Nam left them, jogging quickly back the way they had come. Once he was out of sight, Jaden smiled. "Let's go inside."

"I hope there aren't any more freaks like him in this place," Abree said.

"Nam is a cranky sort, but I assume he's from a bad seed." Jaden turned the latch and pushed.

"A bad seed?"

"Sometimes the experiments don't always work."

"Experiments? Nam is an experiment?"

"Of sorts," he looked beyond her where Nam had disappeared and then grimaced. "So are we. Of sorts."

Suddenly Abree's stomach turned sour. The last thing she wanted to be was an experiment. She took a moment to study Jaden's eyes as he held the door open. She looked for something unnatural in them. Maybe he was a clone or a robot. He acted older than he looked, and he didn't look much older than twelve. His intelligence seemed advanced: his speech precise. He certainly didn't talk like the kids at school, but maybe that was from living underground.

"They're keeping us here to experiment on us?" Abree took a cautious step forward, not sure if she wanted to proceed. "What kind of experiments?"

"Shh!" Jaden peered down the dark hall to their right. "They don't think of it as anything unusual. In fact, they're quite proud of their technology. They want us to feel honored that we're part of their project. What they do in the lab isn't much different than what they're doing outside where you and I came from. Living is just a little more intense down here. They must make sure their technology works before they use it on the masses. I guess we're kind of their guinea pigs, so to speak. Don't tell anyone, but there have been casualties."

Abree's mouth dropped.

"Not for a long time, though. I think they've corrected all the bugs. At least…." his voice tapered and he gave her a questioning glance.

"At least what?" Abree squinted.

"At least I haven't heard of anything else going wrong. Come along. Let's keep moving." A twinge of fear crept through Abree as she watched Jaden latch the door shut.

"Wait a minute. Are you telling me they're going to start experimenting on me?"

"Well, they actually already have."

"And that the Grays are experimenting on people where I live? Like my mom and my brother?"

"It's been going on for a long time. You see? What they're doing is perfectly safe. So safe you didn't even know!"

Abree panicked. "What are they doing?"

"Shh," He held his finger over his lips and led her through a hall that had windows and doorways on either side. "They're doing what we'll be doing. It's not hard. You could enjoy it. It's about mind adjustment."

"Mind adjustment?"

They came to another door that opened out into a tunnel. The minute Abree stepped into the hollow she could smell and taste damp earth. She shuddered. "This is a nightmare. Speaking of which, what happened to Makia?"

"Makia? Who's Makia?"

"The boy who came with me last night. Nam sealed him into a cell. Where is he now?"

"I don't know. I can guess though. Once the Labs arrive, they're divided into sects and the Grays almost never keep new Lab arrivals together. It'd be too dangerous."

"What are you talking about?"

"I guess they think kids from the same neighborhood would get together and cause trouble. You know, revolt or some dumb thing like that. They don't want any gangs coming up with some kind of team spirit." Jaden broke into a quick walk.

"That's crazy. What could we do? The Grays have weapons and cattle prods. I bet they torture people, too. That Nam would," Abree snickered as she jogged to keep up with Jaden.

"Well, I don't think they torture people."

"They hurt Makia his first day here! I saw it."

"Oh, well that was probably a little reminder that Nam is a superior. I'm sure he wasn't damaged."

Abree gaped. "Why are you making excuses for the Grays?"

Jaden turned red in the face and walked even faster. "I'm not making excuses. I'm just saying, you must do what they tell you. They don't ask that much from us. Work mostly."

Abree held her tongue on the issue. Something wasn't right with Jaden and she'd probably be better off not arguing with him. "I don't mind working. I'll do what they ask so they don't torture me, but I'm not going to like it." She slowed, caring little that Jaden rushed on ahead.

He stopped to wait for her, his brow wrinkled into a frown. "Here's the Lab's testing room."

A tall gray building made of metal with strange cloth draped over the exterior stood in front of her. Pipes and cables attached to black boxes hung over the tarp. The ceiling reached to the top of the cave, its angular corners clearly clashing with the natural formation of the underground cavern. There was no way for Abree to tell how deep into the tunnel it went, or if there were other floors beneath.

She studied the peculiar structure as Jaden punched a code into the lock. The door slid open, and then another as they advanced. Jaden touched another control sealing them into a steamy room.

"This is the sterilization room. Put this mask on." Jaden handed her what looked like a gas mask. A long flexible tube attached the mask to a clear globe. Jaden showed Abree how to slip it over her head. As soon as it was buckled in place he attached a cord to her jumper, and one to his. The suits filled with air and then the room filled with steam. Abree's heart raced, but Jaden touched her gently on her shoulder and nodded. The sterilization lasted a few minutes, the suits deflated automatically, and Abree shed her mask when Jaden did.

"That was weird!"

He laughed. "It's odd the first time you do it, but you get used to it after a while."

"Why do we have to have our clothes sterilized anyway?"

"The crops," Jaden answered as he returned the apparatus to their hangers and punched a code into the next lock.

"Crops?"

"They grow food down here." He tossed his chin signaling her to follow him through another passageway. "Once you've gone through vitals, they'll take us to our stations and teach you how to apply the serum to the plants."

"What serum?"

"You'll see."

Abree hurried to keep up with Jaden—more curious now than afraid.

He stopped short and looked around. "Oh no."

"What?"

"I think I took a wrong turn. I get mixed up a lot. We're supposed to be going south, not north."

How he knew north from south down in this hole was beyond Abree. She followed him through another hall.

"This is unfamiliar," he whispered.

"There are cages in these rooms." Abree stopped when she heard a muffled scream. "What was that?"

Jaden's eyes grew as wide as hers. Behind a dimly lit window a group of people in white smocks moved about anxiously and seemed to be wrestling with something on the ground.

"Is that an animal?" Abree asked. "A pig?" Once she heard another shrill scream, she knew her guess was correct. One of the men held up a hypodermic needle filled with blood. She saw the back of a huge pig and heard it grunt as it fought so violently that three other men held it down. She cringed and would have cried out if Jaden hadn't pushed her to the shadows across the hall.

Men inside the room yelled. Something was going terribly wrong.

"The needle broke. Kill it," someone ordered. There was more wrestling and then silence.

"Let's go." Jaden's voice was shaky. He took Abree's hand and they raced down the tunnel. They should have reached the elevator, but instead they passed aisle after aisle of windows, most with shades down, but occasionally Abree could see into a room where rows of cages lined the walls.

"I think—I think these are Labs, Abree. I think this is what we are going to be doing if we survive. Let's get out of here. We aren't supposed to be seeing this."

"What are they doing?"

"I don't know. This part is new to me. I've only worked in the corn lab. We'll have time at lunch to talk. That is if I don't get caught I'm telling you everything."

"You aren't telling me anything." Abree followed Jaden through the labyrinth of halls until they found the elevator. Lost for words, she just stared at her companion as he shot her anxious glances. The elevator dropped down to another floor.

"Not a word about any of this," Jaden whispered. She nodded and followed him through another coded lock way. They stepped into a large vacant room.

"Sign in here," he said handing her a pen and a clipboard that he pulled from the wall. His hands shook, and when he noticed Abree staring at them, he took a deep breath. "Your number, not your name. The Teachers don't know us by name."

"Well, then I'll introduce myself."

"No."

Their eyes locked—his intense, hers anxious.

"I'm not a number. I'm Abree. That's the name my mother gave me and anyone who wants my attention can call me by my name."

"That's not how it works here, Abree. Not with the Teachers. I'll call you Abree when I can, but in the lab and in the testing room, you are 067."

Abree grimaced. Her cheeks turned red. Her eyes darted from the room to the door and back again. Jaden watched her calmly. "You're in this, Abree. There's no getting out of the water but to swim in the river."

She scribbled something illegible on the sheet of paper and handed the clipboard back to Jaden. "Swim in the river, my foot," she said. "Will I ever swim again?"

No sooner were the words off her lips when a door on the far side of the room opened and a group of men and two women entered. They wore jump suits, just like hers. The two women had their hair pulled back in ponytails. One had bright red hair and pale skin, the other looked Hispanic. Abree looked for some sign of kindness written on their faces, but there was none. The men took positions against the wall behind the women, their hands behind their backs. The women approached.

"O42, 067 announce your presence," the red head said.

"Present," Jaden replied, standing at attention, as stiff as the other men. Abree turned to see him salute. He peered from the corner of his eye at her and nodded. She shifted her weight, her eyes narrowed as the woman stepped closer.

"O67 announce your presence," the woman said, her eyes shooting daggers at her.

"You can see I'm here," Abree said. Immediately a volt of electricity stung her shoulder.

"Ow!"

"O67, announce your presence," the woman repeated.

Abree felt the heat race to her cheeks. Another volt stung her left shoulder. "Stop it!"

"Announce your presence 067 or you'll be taken in the back for disciplinary action."

"Abree!" Jaden whispered. "Do it!"

"Present." Abree's voice was barely audible.

The woman smiled slightly and turned, giving way to the dark-haired woman whose eyes reminded Abree of Nathan's friend, Ivana. She looked kind, her features soft, and she walked gracefully, unlike the other woman.

"042, you're released to be with your teachers."

"Thank you, ma'am." Jaden relaxed, giving Abree a sympathetic look before he left the room with his escorts. Abree's heart thumped against her chest, as she stood alone in front of the woman. All her confidence had followed Jaden out the door.

"This is your first day. We'll try to be tolerant of your less than submissive nature. Perhaps you're hungry? This first test must be done on an empty stomach. After that, you and 042 can have breakfast."

"Gee, thanks."

"One thing we will be asking of you is to keep from making comments under your breath. It's disrespectful." The dark-haired woman nodded to the red head. "My assistant isn't nearly as understanding as I am."

"Yes, ma'am." The words came out sour and Abree's lips askew.

"And from now on you can refer to me as Teacher Francis. I'll be your personal tutor and confidant until you graduate."

"And how long might that be?"

"It depends on several things. One of the factors determining your progress is how long it will take to break through your resistance. The other factor is how quickly the nutrients take hold."

Abree said nothing, wishing there were some nutrients to take hold, as her empty stomach growled at the thought of food.

"Your first test is simply a gathering of information you already have in your mind. It shouldn't take long if you're as intelligent as our records say you are." Teacher Francis strolled casually to the right of Abree, her long slender fingers pressed against a set of controls on the wall. Abree jumped back as a metal desk and chair unfolded in front of her, a laptop opened and booted. Teacher Francis ushered her to sit.

"Just answer the questions and you'll be done. The sooner you finish the quicker you'll eat."

The teacher waited for Abree to sit. When she did, a strap automatically buckled around Abree's waist. Teacher Francis then removed a slender case from her belt.

"One more thing," the woman said as she unhinged the case. Resting on a bed of shiny black fabric was a hypodermic needle. "Just a little mind test."

"Mind test?" For an instant Abree saw the pig fighting against the horde of people in the lab. She heard it scream and then she saw it die when the needle broke. Her heart raced as Teacher Francis pricked her skin through a small vent in her suit. Abree squinted and tears trickled past her cheeks, but she refused to cry out. Instead she bit her lip. Teacher Francis attached a tube to the needle and fastened it to a cylinder on the wall. Blood filled the tube and streamed into whatever was on the other side of the panel.

"The sooner you finish your questionnaire, the quicker we'll be able to read your protein." The woman smiled as she walked out the door.

Abree blinked, hoping the pain in her arm would subside and that they wouldn't bleed her to death. A bulleted list of questions popped onto the computer screen. "Name? What do they want? My number? Why don't they just say so," she whispered to herself.

"Answer the question please," a voice from the computer blared, and a red light flashed in the right-hand corner of the screen. *Oh my God, it can hear me!*

Abree entered 067. No way was she going to give this computer her name.

Immediately a new screen appeared with a series of math problems. Easy! Math was Abree's best subject. When she finished the quiz, a buzzer rang out and soon the red-haired woman appeared at the door. "I didn't do anything wrong. I swear!"

The woman laughed, removed the needle, and dropped it into a slot in the wall. With quick hands, she unfastened the strap that held Abree to the desk, gathered the laptop in her arms, and exited to the back room just as Jaden and Teacher Francis entered.

"You're both excused. You may leave for lunch."

Abree rubbed her arm as she followed Jaden out the door, through the sterilization room, and into the halls.

"How did you do?" he asked when they felt free enough to talk.

"That was awful. They poked me and took a ton of blood. Vampires!"

Jaden chuckled.

"What? Why are you laughing? It's criminal!"

"It has to be done. How else would they be able to figure out what food to give you?"

"I don't understand."

"They measure your brain waves and test your blood while you answer the questions. That way they can determine what nutrients you're lacking. Then they provide those nutrients by giving you the right kind of food."

"That doesn't make any sense. Why don't they just serve healthy food and give me anything I want to eat. They have plenty. And I want to know what they're doing with those animals."

Jaden leaned close to her ear. "It's not for you to know what they're doing. Not yet. And there's nothing you can do to stop them anyway. Just be submissive and hope that someday you'll be one of them."

"You know Jaden, I think I'd like you better if you didn't defend them so much."

Jaden's eyes twitched, and he turned away. "How did you do on the test?"

"I aced it. Math is my best subject. Where do we eat? I'm hungry."

"Teacher Francis told me to give you a tour before lunch."

"What? Another tour? I don't think I can handle another tour."

"She thought it would give you a better perspective of this place. She thought that might take some of the sass out of you." His lips turned up at the edges.

"Sass, huh?"

"She makes a point." Jaden's grin broke the ice and they both laughed. With a sweep of an arm he led her through an ascending hallway. "We get to go through the front door this time. I'm kind of excited about it myself."

"This is a different place." Abree squinted from the brilliance as they crested the slope. "The halls weren't this well lit this morning."

"It's the same floor, just a different wing."

The floor was lit with heat lamps that set off a brilliant glow. The walls were cream color, and the tile smooth under their feet. There were rooms with windows on either side of the passageway.

"We're allowed to look in any room that has its blinds open," Jaden said as he stood at the window of a well-lit lab. A young man worked inside unaware of their presence. He stood at a sink washing several hypodermic needles. Behind him a garden bed of corn grew, their leaves reaching a little higher than his shoulders.

"Odd growing crops inside like this. What's wrong with farming the normal way? Like outside where the plants can get sunshine?"

"I've heard they don't want any cross pollination."

"With what?"

"They're experimenting with the genetic makeup of the crops. Here. Read this"

Jaden unfolded a paper he pulled from his pocket and handed it to Abree. She was too fixated on what the boy behind the window was doing to read the pamphlet. "He's taking something out of those petri dishes. What is that stuff? What's he going to do with it?" Abree watched as the boy filled his needle with a slimy pink substance from the glass container. He then held the needle up and walked to the garden, disappearing behind the corn.

"Do you know?" Abree asked.

"No, I don't. But what he's doing is going to be our job too."

"It has something to do with our food, doesn't it? This is how they're changing the makeup of our food, I bet."

"I think you're right, Abree."

"Why? What's wrong with food the regular way? Do you think that serum stuff has anything to do with the animals?"

When Jaden swallowed, his Adam's apple bounced. "I hope not. But we're better off not asking questions. We should just go along with what they tell us. They say we might even get a real bedroom someday if we're good."

"Gee, wow," Abree said. When Jaden looked at her puzzled, she added. "I can hardly wait."

Without another word, he led her back to the lower level and punched a code into the obsidian wall. A great dining hall opened before them. Unlike the lonely halls and vacant cells she had been in, this one was crowded. Being among other people put her nerves at rest, at least for the moment. She returned Jaden's smile and followed him to the cafeteria line. Her stomach growled from the smells.

The food was not recognizable, though the aroma coming from the kitchen suggested toasted grain and spices. Abree mimicked Jaden's choices, but when she reached out to pick up pudding from the buffet, he grabbed her wrist. "Nope. That's not for us," he said. She shook her hand loose from his.

"I love pudding even if it is gray."

"We only get to eat certain foods," Jaden answered, scanning the room as if he were afraid someone had heard them "Only take the food in yellow bowls or plates. That's for us. And don't talk so loudly. There are ears everywhere."

"On people's heads, yeah! What do I care if they hear me?"

"Shh." Jaden led her to a table where three young men sat. They were older, about Nathan's age she guessed, but very muscular. Too muscular—with huge hands larger than any hands she'd ever seen—even larger than Roy Germain's father who worked as a welder. Their speech sounded like Russian, but Abree was no scholar on foreign languages. She sat quietly and listened. The bowls the big men ate out of were blue, and they gulped their food. Their body gestures were animate, and they seemed to be engaged in some sort of disagreement. Once they noticed her staring, they stopped talking, picked up their trays, and left the room. It was then that Abree recognized Makia sitting at a table by the door, alone.

"Oh, my gosh! It's him!" she said to Jaden. "That's the boy I came with on the bus. He's from my school. Are we allowed to talk to each other?"

"We're allowed to associate with whomever we please as long as we're in the lunch room under supervision and monitored," Jaden said. "Why don't you invite him to our table?"

Abree waved to Makia.

"He sees me," she said and waved again. Makia shook his head.

"Something's wrong!" Abree whispered as she set her cup on the table and stood. "What did they do to him?"

"It's hard to say. Be careful," Jaden warned.

"Of what? Makia? What's he going to do to me?"

"I don't know. Lie, maybe? You said he's already been disciplined. That could be a red flag."

Abree tossed her hair. "So? I'd trust Makia before I'd trust any of these jokers!" Without waiting for Jaden's response, she walked to Makia's table, though the boy bowed his head and turned away from her when she arrived. "Why don't you come over and eat with us?" she asked. When he didn't answer, she sat down.

"Are you all right? They didn't hurt you again, did they?"

"Abree," he said, squinting as he peered nervously over her shoulder. "We have to get out of here."

"Come sit with me and Jaden."

"This place is a prison," the boy mumbled. "Everything they do here is wrong. You can't grow crops underground. You can't keep children away from the light. It's all wrong."

"Well, I couldn't agree with you more. But we're here and it doesn't look like we'll be leaving any time soon. Come sit with us." When he looked at her, she saw how circles of worry shadowed his eyes. She felt sorry for him. "Did they hurt you again?"

He shook his head, still scanning the room with suspicious eyes.

"Look, there's got to be some hope somewhere, Makia. Maybe making friends here will help. Jaden seems all right. I think he's one of us. Come and meet him."

She stood and offered him her hand. He gave in, hesitantly, and then slowly followed her. Abree led him directly to her table and offered him a seat across from Jaden. She sat next to him. As Abree ate, Makia stared at her as she moved her fork to her mouth and as she chewed.

"What?" Abree asked, somewhat annoyed by his ogling.

"That's going to change you." Makia finally warned quietly. "You shouldn't eat it."

Jaden cleared his throat. "Don't tell her that. What else are we supposed to eat?"

Abree ignored Jaden and studied Makia's eyes. "What? What do you mean the food will change me? How?" She took another bite. "I'm hungry." It didn't taste very good, but the mash wasn't bitter or anything and it warmed her belly and satisfied her hunger.

His gaze fell on her plate and then to her eyes again. "Be very careful," he warned.

Abree stared back, swallowing the last bite. "Actually, I think you had better eat. I'm sure you're as hungry as I am and it doesn't look like there's anything else to eat. Did they test you too?"

Makia looked at his tray, his brown eyes blank. He nodded his head in such a way it gave Abree a chill. "They took my blood like a vulture devours its kill."

Jaden broke in with a condescending smile. "It wasn't that bad! No more than a blood test, really. You have plenty of hemoglobin left. And they only want to read your protein. Time will pass and you will understand how things operate here. Once you do, life isn't so bad," Jaden took another bite and swallowed. "You'll see."

Makia shook his silky dark locks. "This is not the way of Life. This is all wrong! There's hope, though, a way out. The ant people will show us. I've seen them."

Abree stared at him. "What are you talking about, Makia?" Odd that he would mention ants after she had seen something crawling around in her cell the night before. "What ant people?"

"Ant people? That's ridiculous," Jaden laughed. "Okay, I think I know what's going on with you. They say that new Labs often have nightmares. I've been told it's from being cramped up so close to the walls." He waited, but Makia didn't respond. "Look, if you can't sleep at night, just pretend that your room is like a cocoon. Extra security. You're protected from all the warfare that's going on above ground. That will help you to not feel so claustrophobic. Kind of like a baby blanket. You know what I mean?"

Abree glared at Jaden. "Makia isn't a baby, Jaden. And he didn't have a nightmare. He isn't making anything up."

"Of course, he is!" Jaden laughed again.

Makia's eyes met hers. "It's an ancient legend since the beginning of time. My grandfather told me our legends will someday be real."

Jaden cleared his throat. "Who are your people?"

"The Hopi."

"Look, Makia. I like you so I'm going to clue you in on something. The less you speak about your tribe the better off you'll be. The Grays look at us as just one type of people. There are no more sects and races. So, separate yourself from the idea that you have your own people. We're all your people. Any other way of thinking will get you in trouble."

"Eat, Makia," Abree said gently as she bit into what she thought was bread. "It's not the best food, but it will suffice."

Makia picked up his fork, took a bite and spat onto his plate. He glanced at Jaden and stood. "This isn't food!" With that he walked to the door with his tray and disposed of his dinner. Silence permeated the entire room. His act had not gone unnoticed. Abree held her breath, waiting for something to happen. Makia walked casually to the far wall and leaned against it, his head bowed.

"He'll be punished for that," Jaden whispered to Abree. "If he's your friend, I suggest you go talk to him. He probably should apologize to someone."

She hated the thought of Makia being punished again. "He didn't do anything wrong." She waited a moment, keeping an eye on him and hoping the crowd of people would forget what had happened. Once the stiffness in the air subsided, and people went back to eating and conversing, Abree approached Makia and leaned against the wall with him. "Listen to Jaden," she whispered. "Don't get yourself in trouble again."

He turned to her. "No, Abree. You listen. They're here. Everywhere in the walls, in the floor. When you see them, pay attention to them! They have something to tell you."

"Who?"

Before he could answer her, two men in uniforms barged through the door and stormed up to Makia. They didn't say anything to him, nor to Abree. They grabbed onto his arms and ushered him out of the dining hall. The automatic door sealed shut behind them.

Every head was turned her way and the room grew quiet again. She walked slowly to her table, to her tray, and to the pile of unidentifiable food on her plate. Jaden nodded at her to eat but Abree couldn't bring herself to lift her fork again. Makia's words resounded in her ears. She didn't want to eat the food either, not if it was part of an experiment and especially not after Makia's warning. Who knows what it would do to her? Maybe it might make her hands grow big. The loud speaker came on at that moment.

"067, report to D02," a voice over the intercom said. Jaden sat erect. He set his fork down and stood. "I'll go with you," he offered.

Abree stood and stared at him —speechless. Why was she being summons? Was she going to be punished as well? Jaden took her hand and led her toward the door, slapped his fingers on the controls of the wall, and when it slid open, he led her out of the lunchroom and down the dark halls to a gated elevator.

"Step inside."

Abree's eyes froze wide.

"Step inside, Abree. It's just an elevator. They want to talk to you. I'm sure it's about your friend."

Abree followed Jaden into the elevator, clinging nervously to a rail. The door slammed shut and shot upward so quickly Abree fell forward. Jaden caught and steadied her.

"Don't panic."

The door opened to a hallway much brighter than the one they had just left.

"This way." Jaden rushed her out of the elevator and down another hall.

"What's D02?"

"It stands for Disciplinary Room 2. It's where first time offenders go to be reprimanded. Oftentimes they're allowed a bit of a plea. Maybe your friend asked for you to testify on his behalf."

"Oh."

"Or…." Jaden's pace quickened and he glanced anxiously at her.

"Or what?" The angst in his eyes bothered her.

"Or you could be in trouble, too."

"Great."

The door to D02 opened automatically as they entered within sight of the sensor. Cold white walls surrounded them and in the center of the chamber, Makia sat on the floor. No one else was around.

"042, thank you for escorting 067. You are dismissed. We will inform you of any disciplinary act you must suffer on your charge's account." Surprised, Abree looked around but saw no one else in the room. Jaden pointed to the small surveillance camera above them.

She faced Jaden. "Disciplinary action? You?"

Jaden nodded and swallowed. "Yes. They made you my responsibility so whatever you do, I suffer the consequences. Good luck," Jaden whispered as he pivoted around and left. The door closed behind him. Abree waited, but no other sound came, no instructions from the camera, nothing.

"Well!" she said and looked at Makia. "What did they say to you? What's going on?"

Makia shrugged. "They told me to stay here. Maybe they'll keep me here forever. Why did they bring you?"

"I don't know. Maybe they heard us talking."

"You didn't say anything. I did. All you did was listen to me." He raised his voice, perhaps for the camera. "Here's what I said. I told you not to eat the food. It isn't real. It's poison."

"I know what you told me," Abree whispered. "You don't have to tell the camera."

"I was instructed to repeat what I said once you were here. I'm not ashamed of what I said. It's the truth." Makia leaned forward and whispered, beckoning her to come closer. "If they come to you, do what they do."

"Who?"

He positioned himself between her and the camera, leaning into her ear as she knelt next to him. "The ant people. They're in the walls, in the ground, everywhere. Many forces have tried to oppress them, but always they have resisted. They can teach you how to live among the Grays without becoming their slave."

She studied his eyes. He was serious.

"Promise me you will listen to them and follow their guidance?" he asked.

"Okay. I will. What about you?"

He lifted his hands, his eyes widened with innocence. "This is me.

That's all. I am I. No one else and they won't change me."

"O67 you are finished. Thank you," the speaker blared out, causing Abree to jump. She spun around and stared at the camera.

"Finished with what?"

"155 has transferred the data we were looking for. He's to prepare for the extraction now."

"Extraction?"

"Data removal."

Abree turned to Makia. "Data removal? What are they talking about?"

Makia stood up and stepped away from the corner he had crouched in. With his hands clasped behind his back he set his jaw in defiance. "I think it's over for me. I'm ready."

"Don't say that, Makia. I'll get you out of here."

"Excuse yourself now," the voice blared. The door slid open.

"Go, Abree." Makia's voice was gentle. "Just remember what I told you."

Abree moved to the exit, though she felt like a traitor. Makia stood like a soldier in that cold empty room. Before she could think of a way to grab him and take him with her, the door slammed shut.

It wasn't right. Abree's cheeks burned and her fists clenched. "Makia!" She banged on the wall that had sealed her friend in. "I hate you! All of you!" The walls didn't answer. How could they? They towered over her, sterile, cold, and ruthless. "I hate you!"

The hall door opened. She had a choice to stay and cry, or return to her regimented life. She was doing no good where she was.

❖ ❖ ❖

Makia did not show up at dinnertime, though Abree arrived at the hall early and stayed late waiting for him. She barely touched her food, sick to her stomach over the events of the day. Jaden had no misgivings about what had happened. He ate a healthy portion and ignore her fretting.

"Maybe he's still in that room starving to death." Abree stared at her food.

"No, I doubt it. The Grays don't treat people unjustly. They'll probably keep him in solitary confinement until he learns his lesson. You'll see him again."

"Really? That's what you think? That the Grays don't treat people unjustly?" She studied his eyes, but he kept eating, avoiding hers. "Well, what about those animals we saw? What about that pig they killed?"

"Animals. That's different. I said people."

"What about the pig?"

"Shh."

Abree looked around the room, and when she noticed a couple of children glancing at them she quieted her voice. "What about the animals?"

"I've never known Grays to treat humans the same way."

"I can't believe you're saying that. What are they doing to us? What have they done to Makia? Wouldn't you call this a cage?"

"We have it better off than anyone above ground. Did you forget where we came from? It's a violent world out there right now. The Grays are saving us from torment and murder."

His words drove nails into Abree's heart. Her mom was in that world. Her brother. "I suppose I should be thankful for being rescued by them. From them, shouldn't I?" Abree scoffed, remembering her brother's warm and comforting hand being ripped from hers before the Gray soldiers pushed her onto the bus.

"You should. Soon they'll be giving you food in your room. Tasty food. Sweet, like candy. The more you eat, the better an attitude you'll have."

"You mean, the more complacent I'll become?"

"Call it what you may. You'll settle into the order of things as time goes on."

"Is that what's happening to you? Are you eating their candy?"

He didn't answer; neither did he look at her.

"Settling" was not Abree's plan. She wished she had the same courage Makia had. She stopped eating at that moment, and set her fork down on her tray. She could go on a hunger strike, but it would be hard. She lacked that kind of discipline. Not only did food tempt her, but also, she had grown to like going to the dining hall. It was the only place she could talk to anyone.

❖ ❖ ❖

Abree didn't sleep that night. Her stomach growled from hunger but at the same time she was nauseous. Jaden had warned her that the food might make her stomach upset for a few days. *"Sometimes the new diet takes time to get used to,"* he had told her. He wasn't kidding.

She closed her eyes to avoid the vertigo, and saw her mom's flowerbed at home.

"I really should just stay and water them," she whispered to herself. "I worry too much. I should just take care of the things that I have." Abree opened her eyes. " Oh dear! Why am I thinking of flowers in such a dark and creepy room. But then," she reasoned to herself, "this place isn't all that creepy. It's like a cocoon. Like being under a nice warm blanket on a cold and chilly day." The thought comforted her. "I kind of like being here!"

And then she heard Makia's voice in her head. "No! The food will make you complacent." Makia's words resonated in her mind. "The ant people. They're in the walls, in the ground, everywhere. They can teach you how to live among the Grays without becoming their slave," he had said, and she whispered his words again.

"Teach me what?" She laughed. "I don't want to learn anything. I just want to hang out and do what the Grays tell me to do. I'll be fine."

She saw the red feelers emerging from the cracks in the floor, inching into her cell room--an ant scurrying aimlessly about.

"No. Makia's wrong. He's a rebellious boy and I shouldn't listen to him. He'll get me in trouble." She blinked again, waking herself to reality as her stomach growled. "It's the food, isn't it? I'm seeing things. I'm dying.

I'm dead. I'm dead and the bugs have come to eat my body." She sat up on the bed. *Makia is right. The food is poison. It's warping my thoughts!*

There were ants in her room. They crept through the crack near her bed. One of them tugged at a grain of food he carried, rolling and skirting upward, catching its burden frantically before it dropped into the dark. Another ant eased back into the crack and soon tackled the same load. Eventually the two lifted a kernel of corn into Abree's room and carried it across the floor. Their path meandered in senseless direction, or so Abree assumed, until they disappeared into a narrow crevice in the wall.

Abree waited, hoping they'd return. "How crazy silly. I'm supposed to learn from that? Two little bugs scrambling around, carrying a dumb old grain of corn. What is that teaching me, Makia? Even the ants have gone wild over corn! This whole stupid community is about corn. The reason I'm down here in this hole in the ground is so that I can work in some secret room filled with corn. The reason you're in prison, Makia, is because you won't eat corn. And now the ants are getting in on the action and stealing it. Did you hear that, Makia? The ants are stealing corn! Is that what I'm supposed to do? Right!" She snickered and rolled over, refusing to think about ants again.

Confiscation

"Did you see this, Nathan? Did you see it?" Molly slid the glass door open, holding an envelope in the air. Nathan dodged for the basketball that bounced on the patio and turned to his mother. Her face flamed red with anger.

"Now what, Mom?"

"It's a notice to abandon the house. They're taking our home away."

"What?" He jumped up the porch steps and took the papers from his mother's shaking hands. The words were plain and simple, but Nathan refused to believe them. "It's a joke." He followed his mother inside.

"It's a highway. It says right there. The Grays are claiming the neighborhood. We have a week. One week. Good God, son, what am I going to do?" She collapsed on a chair at the dining room table and buried her head into her hands as she sobbed. "First my baby girl, now this."

"Mom," Nathan skimmed through the papers. "No. This is insane! They can't take our home and everything you've ever worked for. No compensation? Nothing? I don't get it? Are these people human?"

"Read the fine print. They're giving me an option. I get to move into one of their nursing homes."

"Nursing home? Mom, you don't need a nursing home. You aren't old. There isn't anything wrong with you!"

"No?" Tears ran down her cheeks. "I didn't think so either, but I'm beginning to wonder."

Nathan slammed the papers on the table and slapped his fist into his hand to keep from putting a hole in the wall.

"Stop it Mom, don't put yourself down. And don't cry! They aren't going to take the house away. We'll get with the neighbors and file a lawsuit. We'll get to the bottom of this."

"This is the bottom, Nate."

"No. There has to be a way out. You're too young for a nursing home!"

"Didn't you read the letter? It has nothing to do with how old I am. They're offering me a place to stay because they're taking my house. I guess there's some good in their system after all. At least they aren't throwing me out on the street."

Nathan's heart broke for his mother. He moved a chair next to hers and put his arm around her. She buried her head in his shoulder. "What's happened, Mom? All the fight has gone out of you. They're breaking your spirit. You can't let them do that. You can't give in."

She pulled a napkin from the table and blew her nose. "There's not much to fight with anymore, son. They've taken all my ammunition. I guess I've arrived at a place where I see I can't win." She tossed her hands half-heartedly. "So, I surrender."

"No!"

"It happens in every war, son. Someone wins and someone loses. You can't always win. Remember that. We can't always win. Not when we're so outnumbered."

"I'm not accepting that."

"No? Read that last page." She pushed the papers that lay on the table closer to him. "You have a chance to get out of this hole. There's an application to enlist. Join the Enforcers. They want you. Look, they mentioned your name. They think you'd make a good engineer and officer. This is your chance, our chance. You join, Nathan. They'll be good to you. They'll give you a home, food, education, and a job. I can go to the nursing home."

"Mom, that's ludicrous."

She stood, straightened her skirt against her waist, and wiped her eyes. Molly always dressed professionally, her hair curled in place, lipstick the perfect color for her complexion. There was nothing about her that warranted a nursing home.

"What about your job?" Nathan asked.

Their eyes locked with a look of dismay in Molly's.

"I don't have a job."

Nathan's mouth dropped. "What?"

"The Grays have brought in their own court system. All the lawyers have been dismissed. I was laid off this morning. We've lost the war, Nathan."

His family was dissolving before his eyes. His sister had been gone a month already and every day he grieved at the loss. He missed her freckled cheeks and silly pout. Of course, Mom was even more distressed over Abree's absence. No word had come from his sister at all. No word of any of the children in the neighborhood. Parents were distraught, but there was no one to lash out at, no one to answer questions. The Grays that had taken them away were gone, on to some other city.

"Where is the mayor?"

"The mayor? That's a joke! A high-ranking officer of the Privatol Army stands looking over the mayor's shoulder. The police now have a Gray police chief; the guard's uniforms have been changed to gray. Can't you understand? It's martial law over the entire country. Gray coats sit in the district offices-men that neither you nor I can even understand, much less appeal to."

"Where are they from?"

"I'm not sure. They have a Mongolian dialect, but I believe they are Russian. It doesn't matter where they're from. They've infiltrated our system. Our community is one of the last ones they've conquered and they did so right before our eyes. First the gasoline prices, the local government, then the schools. Now the homes are being confiscated and all of this within the boundary of our own laws, until our laws were swallowed up in their tyranny. It's over."

Molly walked to the hallway and stood silent for a moment before she spoke. "I'm going to pack. Think about it. Other families are surviving because they have stopped resisting change. Mr. Garcia has joined the Grays, and look how his family has benefited. No one is allowed out of the country, but he acquired privilege for his family. They're all in Mexico now. Maybe they'd let you do something like that. Maybe you could get Abree back to us?"

"Do you even want to live in Mexico?" he asked quietly, skimming through the papers again.

She shook her head. "No, but if it meant freeing Abree…."

"I don't see any deal like that in here."

"Maybe you could talk to them. Maybe if they like how you work?"

Nathan slammed his fist on the table and stood, unable to hold his anger any longer. "Damn it, Mom!" She spun around, wide eyed at his outburst as his chair fell over. "What leverage would I have that they'd make a deal with me? I'm a kid. Mr. Garcia has been an engineer all his life. Of course, they asked him to join. Of course, they let Ivana and her aunt go to Mexico. They aren't going to set Abree free because I enlisted. And I'm not signing any contract to join the Enforcers."

"You're still a minor. You do what I tell you."

"Mom! No." Nathan never raised his voice at his mother before, but he refused to succumb to the Privatol and its coercion. "I'm not doing it. I can't. I don't want you to be in a nursing home and how can I enlist? Look what they're doing to everyone. People we know! People I grew up with. My friends. Your friends! Look what they do to protesters. Do you want me on the other end of that? Carting my friends off in a swat truck at gunpoint? Do you want me to shoot them? Is that what you want for my life?"

She buried her head in her hands, fell on the couch, and sobbed.

"You do what you feel is right Mom, but I'm packing my bags and I'll be out of your way. Tell them I left. Tell them I'm a runaway."

"You'll be a criminal."

"I already am. We're all criminals. They're imprisoning all of us.

That nursing home will be a prison for you. Mexico would be a prison for you. The only choice I have is to stand up for what I believe. It doesn't matter if they hunt me down and shoot me. I'm not falling into their trap. I'm not joining them." With that he stormed through the house grabbing clothes from the laundry basket, his backpack, his hunting knife and a slingshot.

"Nathan, listen to reason."

"Reason? What reason did they give you for taking your house? Because they want your son?"

"You're a smart boy. Of course they want you."

"They want all the boys my age so that no one is left to contest them. We're a threat to them in numbers, so they coerce our families into giving us away." He slammed his fist into the wall bursting through the sheet rock. "Well, I have news for them. They can't have me. I'll never be one of them. Not if it kills me." He kicked at the wall busting more sheet rock.

She burst into tears. Nathan rubbed his fist from the pain.

"Mom, don't. I'm sorry. I shouldn't have yelled at you like that." He quickly raced to her side and knelt next to her, taking her hands in his. "I don't mean to break your heart. I'm not against you. I love you. I want to protect you. Just come with me and let me take care of you."

She wiped her eyes and looked at him. Her curls clung to her cheeks from all the tears that rolled over them. She took his head in her hands. "I want to see you grow up, Nathan."

"Come with me, then."

"Where to?"

"I don't know. And if I did I wouldn't tell you. The less you know the safer it is for you. Mom, please. Don't go to that nursing home."

"I'm going to the home, Nathan. I don't have the fight in me that you do. If I could persuade you to enlist I would, just to see you live to a ripe old age."

"As a Gray? Never."

"They'll hunt you down and kill you."

"No, Mom. I'll hide. They won't find me." Nathan rose and slung the pack on his back, his heart aching, but finding no other solution but to flee. "I'll go right now. They won't know or suspect it now. They'll wait until the day they take you away and then ask for me, but I won't be here. I'll be gone."

He hated seeing her with her hands clasping her face, red from trauma, tears rolling down her cheeks, but he made his decision. "Please come with me."

A long moment passed before she answered. "I can't."

"I love you, Mom. If I find a safe place for us I'm coming to get you, nursing home or not."

She nodded and smiled through her tears. "Look at you. Such a courageous young man—standing up for what you believe in. I'm proud of you and I love you. I will always love you." Her voice trailed into exhaustion as she fell back on the couch.

Nathan left, shutting the door silently behind. Maybe his actions were too hasty, but this might be his only chance to escape. He'd find a way out and come back for his mom.

Mexico

Ivana stepped off the train, her head still rumbling from the ride. Though deep into the night, the hot air offered no relief from the stuffy cabin car she'd been riding in. Only a few passengers disembarked with her. Del Rio was not a popular township, having a history of heavy cartel activity. Only policemen and a few struggling merchants and their families living at the mercy of the drug lords remained. Ivana hated that she had to get off at this station, but rail stops were few along the border of Mexico.

"Vana!"

"Thank the Blessed Mary you're here," Ivana called to her brother as he jogged along the tracks. Auntie Flora followed, hunched over, holding her scarf close to her neck. She leaned heavily on a wooden cane and struggled to keep up.

"José." Ivana swung her arms around him. His dark sun-kissed skin creased into a smile. Only a few years older than she, José was stout and handsome, his strong jaw set in a perpetual grin. His words immediately mixed with her auntie's as they spoke a collage of greetings in Spanish. They hugged Ivana between tears.

"Auntie Flora, José, please, enough kisses! Let's go. Let's get out of here," Ivana broke away finally. "This place gives me the creeps."

"We were so worried about you, Vana," Aunt Flora said through tears as they walked. "I wanted you to leave the States when I did, but your father insisted on waiting."

"I had to finish the semester."

"Oh school, yes. I know, but the rumors here fly around like the swallows. We're so far away from my brother, and so little word comes to us. We don't know what to believe. Your father didn't write. Nothing. I haven't heard from him so we worried something wicked had happened."

Ivana and José exchanged glances: hers troubled, his unrevealing. Her father did send word. She knew because she had helped him write the letters in Spanish.

"Auntie, that's not so...." she started, but José interrupted.

"Let's get out of here," he whispered. "Our grandfather is home alone and waiting for us."

"How is Papi?"

"Still tilling the soil. Hurry to the truck. There are too many ears. Sometimes the police will question us." He threw an anxious glance at Ivana, ushering her and Aunt Flora into the dark, away from the station, nodding toward his truck lit only by starlight. "Quickly."

"Screw the police. I won't tell them anything." Ivana jogged after her brother.

"They'd make you." José tossed the luggage into the bed of his old primer-gray pickup and opened the door for their aunt, assisting her into the cab. Ivana jumped in next to her and slammed the door. "Whatever you remember about Del Rio, it's ten times worse now," he added.

"José, Papa did write...."

"It's a long ride back, Ivana." José cut her off again. "Long enough to tell us all that you've been doing in school."

"School?" She frowned and looked at her brother. Aunt Flora sat in between them. Shorter than the two siblings, her colorful scarf draped over her dark hair gracefully. Though fast approaching old age, she had a youthful beauty about her.

José scowled back. "Shh," he cautioned silently and nodded toward their aunt.

Ivana bit her lip. Maybe there will be a better time.

The tires spun, shooting a cloud of dust into the air when José threw the truck in reverse.

"Hey, brother. Chill!" Ivana warned, but he ignored her and burned rubber as they headed out of town. Seeing that he passed the road leading to the cluster of adobe houses where she grew up, Ivana turned to him. "Where are you going?"

"We moved. We don't live in town anymore. It's too dangerous. We're at the farm. Papa didn't tell you?"

"Papi's farm?"

He nodded. Steadying his hand on the wheel. "*Si.*"

"You fixed the house up out there?"

"We have a special room for you, Vana. You'll stay with us now?" Aunt Flora asked.

"Maybe for a week or two, but I'm going back to the States to get my degree. I'm just here to visit. I told you that. There are things I need to do at home. Don't worry Auntie; the Privilege Clause is good for a few years. I'll be back."

"What things do you need to do? What's more important than your life?" Aunt Flora pouted. "You should stay here. My brother told me to keep you safe. Why do you go back? There's nothing for you there."

"One more year, that's all. I promise." Ivana wasn't sure she could keep that promise. Still, it would ease her aunt's mind. "What I'm learning is important. I'm studying political science. The world needs people like me. Even if this new government in the States, the Privatol, is successful they still need people who think deep, who are educated. And if not, the others may need a leader." She shrugged—a wry smile crossed her face. José shot her a questioning look.

"You walk dangerously Vana," he said. Aunt Flora's eyes darted between the two.

"You're just like your father, Vana. You jump off all the cliffs into the deep waterholes, never knowing if you will swim or hit your head on a rock." Aunt Flora adjusted the scarf on her head.

"Where's the thrill though, if you never jump?" Ivana asked.

"Bah!" Aunt Flora waved at her, as though her gesture would clear such thoughts from her niece's mind. "Just stay and work the soil with us."

Ivana didn't answer. She could settle into a peaceful life on a farm when she gets old, but not now. She'd seen too much of the world's suffering. Papa needed her— her friends needed her—and the twins needed her to rescue them. The long train ride had allowed her time to think. As much as she wanted to get away from the political oppression the United States was experiencing, there had to be something she could do to help. It was only a matter of time before the Privatol would be targeting Mexico. Maybe she'd be able to find and save all her loved ones. Maybe someday the whole family could move to the farm.

"I can't stay here, Auntie. Didn't Papa tell you? They took the twins. It happened right after you left."

José swore and pounded his fist on the steering wheel.

Aunt Flora gasped. "Oh, those dear sweet babies!" Her voice cracked. She shook her head and gasped more than once, the tears in her eyes sparkled in the moonlight. "Not the babies!"

"They're seven years old, now, Auntie."

"How did it happen?" José asked.

"Just like routine." Ivana reached for her purse and dug through it looking for her gum. "Just like they do everything. They tell you they are coming and then they come." She unwrapped a stick of mint and put it in her mouth, tossing the wrapper back in her bag. "You have to obey. You don't know who they'll kill if you don't. Maybe you. Maybe them. Maybe some complete stranger."

Auntie shuddered. "And you want to go back to that?"

"I want to change it."

"How? You're no magic woman. How?" José shot her a glare.

The rumble of the tires across the desert road shook the cab. Ivana didn't doubt the anger mounting in José. Usually peaceful, his temper flared when the family was in harm's way. Dust filtered through the window cracks as his foot fell heavy on the gas pedal.

Ivana's thoughts were on the home she just left. The little town called Sunrise, her mom and papa. She missed the twins. As rowdy and undisciplined as they were, she loved her younger siblings. Tears welled in her eyes. She fought them. "It's hard to talk about it," she said, hoping José and her auntie would understand her sorrow, "but it would be better if we have a discussion. Maybe we could come up with a plan."

"No plans," her brother responded abruptly.

She turned to him. "You don't mean that."

He didn't answer, but his set jaw and narrowed eyes told her he did.

The desert flew by. Stars were out and Ivana fixed her gaze on them. She rolled down her window. A slight drop of temperature met her brow as the wind blew her hair and dried her sweat. The wide-open country smelled good. There was space out there. Space that separated her from pain and sorrow and worry. The rising moon played games with her mind as it seemingly danced from one window to the other. She felt like a child again and then her spirits fell. Why should she be so lucky to feel the wind and breathe the desert air when the twins, and Nathan's family, and all the kids from school were in the hands of the most dangerous men in the world?

She inhaled her fear and watched José, his countenance stern as he drove.

Aunt Flora's head fell on her shoulder and the woman snored. Still beautiful despite her age, Papa had often said Ivana was born in the image of his sister. Ivana pushed a black curl from the woman's forehead and kissed her. It was good to be in Mexico again, if only for a short while.

José cleared his throat, glancing at their aunt before he spoke. "I got the letters from Papa. She doesn't know."

Ivana frowned. "Why? Why didn't you tell her? She worries too much already."

"It's for her safety. If they ever question us, she won't have to lie."

"Question us about what? What are you talking about? Who are they? What's going on that I don't know?"

"Papa's letters."

"I read them. There isn't anything secret in them. He talked about the farm a little."

"His words were short, but they meant more."

"What do you mean?"

His dark eyes caught hers. "He didn't tell you, did he?"

"Tell me what?"

"What he's doing."

Ivana shrugged. "He joined the Enforcers. It's not something I'm proud of, but it got us privilege. A sort of sacrifice, I guess."

José was still looking at her, taking only brief glimpses at the road ahead. "Yes, it is a sacrifice." His face shone as red as an adobe oven. "That's the very least that it is!"

"Well, he didn't ask us if that's what we wanted, to have him turn traitor on our behalf."

"You listen to me, Ivana. Papa is not a traitor. Do you understand?"

"What do you call it then?"

"Just shut up about it. You don't know anything."

"He's arresting people. He's shipping them off to concentrations camps or wherever it is they go."

"You don't know that, so just shut up."

"He wears a uniform. People call him a Gray."

"Shut up, I said!"

Aunt Flora stirred.

"Shut up. Yeah, I'll shut up." Ivana faced the window. She hated fighting with José; he had such a bad temper.

She could smell the river now. If the sun were up she'd see the cottonwoods, but in the dark, there were only shadows at the base of the hills to indicate the meandering Rio Grande. José slowed the truck as it rocked across the poorly graded road, enough so that she could hear bullfrogs and crickets. What a sweet melody.

"It's been a long time since I heard that sound," she said, hoping she could calm her brother's rage.

"You could hear it for the rest of your life if you weren't so damn stubborn."

"Yeah? Well, stubborn runs in the family."

The truck stopped in front of the house. No neighborhood, only a small shanty made of adobe and a log roof. Several out-buildings dotted the landscape and a barbed wire fence behind them needed fixing. Two barking dogs greeted them as a light brightened the window.

Ivana stepped out of the cab as Aunt Flora jolted awake.

"Home!" the woman said. "And Papi's up."

"Papi?" Ivana was thrilled at seeing her grandfather again. By all rights the man should be in his grave. No one knew his age, only his wrinkled smile. He opened the door and Ivana rushed to greet him.

"Vana, the rose of Heaven!" he said in broken English as she stole a hug from him. Though Papi stood a foot shorter than Ivana, his size was in his character. He patted her on the back. "Come in. Eat. Put meat on those bones. Too long we don't see you. What do I have to do, worry? They starve my *nieta* in the land of plenty?"

She laughed and followed the old man into the house, the dogs at her heels jumping at her and wagging their tails. José followed with the luggage and held the door for Aunt Flora.

"Eat. You're as thin like the ants." Papi pulled a chair away from the table.

"Papi, it's the fashion. Too much fat and the boys don't look at you," Ivana laughed. She took a place at the table. "Did José make this furniture? Last time I was here you had nothing but a card table."

"José? *Si*, with little help from his Papi, he's not too bad." The old man tapped his brow and grinned.

"Nice job, brother!" Ivana laughed. José nodded thanks.

Aunt Flora excused herself, stepping into one of the bedrooms. Papi set some tortillas and beans on the table and signaled for Ivana to eat. José joined her as their grandfather watched.

"In all my years, I have never heard of such bad things in the States."

Papi pulled up a chair next to Ivana. "Even during the war." He shook his head slowly. "This is not what your Papa dreamed. No fortune. It is a prison. Tell us more. What do you see?"

"I don't know any more than what Papa knows." She stole a peek at José, wondering if Papi knew about their father's betrayal. Her brother's expression was cold, his eyes daring her to tell.

"I heard they poison the food?"

Ivana stopped chewing and studied the old man's face. "Why do you say that? It's just food alteration. Not poison and it's nothing new. Why?"

"NCF your father says. What is that?"

"Newly Constructed Food? It's their method of improving the crops, so to speak, to make more food for more people. The Gray's food altering situation is hardly a concern for us. There are more oppressive things that they do...."

"You agree with this process?"

"We learned about the process in school. I don't agree with them, but I can choose what I eat, can't I?"

"Maybe that's why you're so skinny."

Ivana blushed. "No, Papi. That's not why I'm so skinny." She broke off a piece of her tortilla and dipped it in her beans. Papi pushed his chair from the table and stood, walked to the stove, and picked up the kettle. His movements were slow but steady.

"I'm surprised that the Grays aren't down here doing the same thing that they've done in the States. What keeps them away?" Ivana asked.

"The Cartel." José leaned back in his chair.

"Seriously? The drug lords that terrorize our towns?"

"They won't let them near the border. There have been shootouts and murders. No one sides with the Grays without losing a family member. As bad as the Cartel is, they like their traditions and they hate the Grays. And they don't want anyone messing with their food or their territory."

Papi set a cup of hot cocoa in front of Ivana and took a seat next to her. "Men cannot improve what *Dios* gives us, Flower. You know that, don't you?"

"Papi, it's Science. The good Lord gave us our minds too, didn't he?"

"*Si*. To choose his ways."

Ivana laughed. "Okay. Whatever you say."

Papi shook his head, staring at the tortillas. "You will live better when you listen to wisdom, so listen to our saying."

"What saying?" Ivana asked, a smile on her face. She loved the old man regardless of his preaching. Papi never thought twice about getting to the point.

"All we have is our fields, our seed, and our home. Come in peace, till the ground with us."

Ivana nodded, not sure of the implications of his words. "That's a good saying, Papi." She wiped her mouth with her napkin and looked at his twinkling eyes. His teeth sparkled. "So, you want me to help you plant your fields?"

His smile eased. Such gravity on his face was unusual. "*Si*. Your father has told me much more. Maybe he hasn't told you. What the men of this Gray Army do to food is not a good thing. Do they think they are the Gods?"

"It seems that way. It's not the farmer's fault, Papi. The military. It's the men in uniform who are taking over." She eyed her brother who had been staring at her. Does Papi know that his son is wearing one of those uniforms? "Maybe you're right. Maybe they're all trying to be Gods."

"They think they are the winged serpent that has come to save the world?"

"What winged serpent? Oh," she laughed, remembering the childhood stories. "You mean Quetzalcoatl? You don't believe in that legend still, do you?"

"You don't?"

She set her fork down. Her grandfather had not taken his eyes off her. Neither had her brother.

"It would be good to remember. The stories of your people are not fairytale."

Ivana sneered, and then relented. She was in Mexico now. Tradition had not been compromised here. "I'll listen, Papi."

"There was another world before ours. Even your scientists know. Quetzalcoatl survived the destruction of that world. When all was done, he took his blood and mixed it with clay." Papi spat on his hands, clapped them together and rubbed his arms. "He stirred this mixture of blood and clay with the bones from men who died."

Ivana bit her cheek to keep from smiling. Papi was serious.

Papi tapped his forehead, a scowl on his face. "Science. Just like your NCF."

If the candles hadn't been casting eerie shadows on both the men's faces, Ivana may have laughed, but her grandfather's words were haunting, and she felt like a little child again, listening to a ghost story.

"Okay. Then what happened after that?"

"What do you think? Suddenly Quetzalcoatl had a million people at his knees. He had to feed them or they would die. Just like a mother with *los niños*, he loved them. But where to find food for such a crowd? Ah! Quetzalcoatl had sharp eyes. He saw a red ant, scurrying across the ground with a kernel of corn in his jaws."

"Ah! Yes, the ant people? The ones who know enough to put food away for winter."

Papi's smile broke free. "Now you remember! Good. Quetzalcoatl stopped the ant and asked, 'Where do you get this corn I see'? But the red ant...." Papi shook his head and pouted. "He wouldn't say. Maybe he doesn't trust Quetzalcoatl. He said, 'You will make me a slave to bring food to a million people!' I don't know."

"Still, the ant's resistance didn't stop our dragon friend though, did it, Papi?" José laughed.

Papi chuckled. "No. Our dragon is like the Cartel." Papi gave José a curt glance. "A bully. *Azcatl,* the ant, finally took Quetzalcoatl to the volcano, the opening to the Earth. The dragon was too big to go where the ant went, so he had to change into an ant. Dyed black by the coal under the Earth, he became a black ant. He followed Azcatl through the narrow cracks in the mountain. Deep inside, Quetzalcoatl discovered the corn. Azcatl let Quetzalcoatl take some to his people. The dragon chewed on the maize to make mash and then fed it to the little people and then they grew. The rest of the seed they planted."

Ivana laughed. "That's a crazy story, Papi."

The old man nodded. His cheeks curled when he smiled, giving his eyes a happy shape. "Crazy. *Si.*"

"But what does it have to do with me?"

His smile sobered. He looked her dead in the eye. "Your father is the red ant."

Ivana sat up straight, her focus darting between Papi and José. "What do you mean?"

"For several years, the seed for our farms has only come from America. There is no other seed," José said. "No one here thought anything of it, until our father sent us news about what the Grays are doing to that seed."

"News?"

"Papa's not a traitor, Vana. He works for them, yes, but not to help them. He's put himself in danger so that he can help us. He goes to meetings with them. He works underground with them. He sees how the Grays are manipulating the world supply of food to breed people. It is subtle. No one knows what happens to them until it is too late."

"They breed people?"

"A complicated process, more complicated than what you learned in school, but it comes down to breeding, yes."

"So, what does Papa do?"

"He's smuggling seed to our farm. Good seed. Seed from deep under the ground where the storehouses are."

"Oh, Mother Mary!" Ivana drew in her breath, absorbing the news. "Then he's working as a double agent?"

"We grow the crops, feed our family, store some grain and send the rest south. Every year we'll harvest a different crop. This year corn. Next year wheat maybe. You must never tell anyone Papa's role. Not even Aunt Flora."

"But why are you telling me?"

José moved uncomfortably in his chair. Papi stood. "I will let you two talk now." His grin prompted a smile from Ivana.

"Good night, Papi. Rest well."

"It's good to have you home, Flower."

They watched Papi move quietly into the sleeping room and snuff out the candle.

So many questions spun in Ivana's head, and the long trip had made her weary, but José's anxiousness suggested there was more that he wanted to tell her, and that she should know. So, she waited.

"So why are you telling me this?" she asked after Papi shut the bedroom door.

José breathed deeply and adjusted the wick of the lantern higher. The flame scorched the tip of the globe with a dark residue.

"Just so that I know? Or is there another reason?"

"You need to know."

"What, then? Why do I need to know the details about Papa's smuggling? Does he want me to help him? What?"

"He doesn't want you to go home. He fears you'll be a target of interrogation if he gets caught."

He wants me to stay here?"

"Yes."

"And farm?"

José looked at her, his expression hopeful.

Ivana laughed. "I'm not a farmer, José. I'm a student. I have a career ahead of me. Maybe I'll be a politician someday. Maybe the world needs me, like they need Papa." When José didn't respond, she laughed again. "That's crazy. I can't stay here and farm. I'd just cause trouble for you."

"You could help Aunt Flora. She's getting old. She can't keep up with all the work here."

"I love Aunt Flora, but I'd go crazy staying here all the time. No," Ivana shook her head. "No, José. You know I love it here, but I love it in America, too. Even if it is getting hard to live there, I must help. I have friends there. The twins are there. Papa is there and so is Mama. How can I leave them?"

"Papa will be sending Mama home soon. He's working on a deal now."

"Mama's consenting?" Ivana's mother told her once she would never return to Mexico. José shrugged.

Ivana sat in silence thinking about the prospect of staying. It didn't seem right. She wasn't a homemaker and everyone in the family would expect her to cook and take care of things the way her mom and auntie do, but that wasn't the reason she didn't want to stay. There was a passion for justice that was bubbling inside of her. Ivana was an activist, an outspoken student who wanted to make a change in the world and there was so much of the world now to change. Hiding on a farm was not the answer to the world's problems. Not now, anyway.

"I won't be content, José. I'll be miserable."

"It's not just about you, Vana. It's about keeping our entire family safe. It's about growing some seed that's natural and real for neighbors to grow and to send on to other parts of the world."

"Yeah. Yeah, it is. And you and Papi are doing a fine job of that. You don't need me. I don't know anything about farming. I do know about politics, though. If someone doesn't stop the Grays, then you won't have a farm to grow anything on. They'll come here and they'll find you, and when they do, they'll slaughter you. Your little cartel isn't going to stop them."

His face showed trouble and resentment. "You think you can stop the entire Privatol Army?"

Ivana shrugged. She wanted to. She could at least help her father. "I'll be here for two weeks. That's it. I'm not leaving my family until they can come with me. And I'm finishing school in the fall. After that, we'll see."

All José did was nod several times, sending daggered looks Ivana's way. She could tell he was mad, but it didn't matter. Nothing he could say would convince her to stay in Mexico. There were too many people to save.

"We'll talk about this again, Vana. In the meantime, think. Think really hard about what's going to happen to you if you get arrested." He pushed his chair from the table. The sound startled Ivana and she jumped. One last glare and José stepped outside and slammed the door.

❖ ❖ ❖

Sleeping in another bed away from home in the summer time had never been something Ivana did comfortably. She was used to the constant hum of the swamp cooler in her father's house, a sound that would lull her to sleep while drowning out the horrors of the nocturnal city. Here on the farm the silence was too loud. Her ears hurt from lack of hearing. She lay awake, looking through the screen of the window, watching the stars turn into visions of uniforms and school buses.

The oppression of the Grays, though far away, haunted her. The damage her homeland had suffered left a wound in her heart too painful to ignore. A tear streamed down the side of her face just before the dark world of sleep took her.

"Ivana!" the voice whistled, sounding much like the wind blowing through a reed, first distant and then shrill. "You know where they are. Tell me. Show me. Take me to them."

Ivana's heart raced with fear and her eyes flew open. "Who are you?" The room was lit with a brilliant flame. Before her stood the strangest creature. Blue, green, and red feathers danced around the head of a dragon. Its eyes sparkled and yellow and white sparks flew from its teeth. Ivana gasped.

"Take me to them!" Its voice shook the room.

"Who? Take you to whom?" She trembled, unable to tell if she were awake or not.

"The red ones. The Ant people."

"What are you talking about?"

The creature didn't stay around to explain. As soon as it had spoken, it evaporated into the air leaving Ivana breathless.

"Papi?" There was no one awake that she could tell. A gentle breeze blew through the open window. The moon was high overhead, its light glistening on the poplar tree at the end of the drive. A coyote howled in the distance, but other than the night sounds, nothing stirred. Ivana put on her robe and stepped into the hall where a lantern flickered on the wall.

"Papi?" She didn't want to wake him. Still, she wished he were there to explain the vision.

"Ivana? What are you doing up?" José peeked out from his room.

"I had a dream, I think." She hesitated to tell him more when she saw his crooked smile.

"A dream? You've had a long trip and are over-tired. Don't wake Papi tonight for a child's dream. Go to sleep. I'll make sure they won't come and get you." His laugh was teasing, but it hurt.

"Of course!" Ivana said and slipped back into her room. It wasn't just a child's dream. It was the Quetzalcoatl, and Papi would know more. All she had to do was survive the night and talk to him in the morning.

On Top

Nathan slept in the woods that night, anxiously waking at every snap of a twig or call of a night owl that perched on a branch of the ponderosa pine near his head. His uneasiness came not only from fear that he might open his eyes to shiny black boots and a rifle cocked and aimed at his head, but from having left his mother in a vulnerable position. The walk to the woods beyond the golf course had been long and grueling. Not only was the day hot, but the hill steep, his pack heavy, and the streets constantly patrolled by Grays. Dodging into the brush cost him a few scratches from prickly bushes, and a scrape or two from tree limbs, but the pain was nothing compared to the remorse he felt leaving his mother alone. Returning, however, would not be wise. He made his decision, now he had to live with it. His mom had to live with it, too.

Nathan woke before dawn, giving up on sleep. He knew of a ravine nearby where the ground was soft and open enough for a shelter. It was there he dug, having packed his folding shovel. Most of the ground was mulch made up from years' worth of rotting fiber. Damp leaves and crumbling wood mixed with dark earth afforded him a burrow supported by the roots of an old maple tree.

Satisfied it was deep enough, Nathan rested for only a moment. The sky caught color from the rising sun, reminding him that there was no time to waste. Nathan gathered the largest logs he could find and built a roof, testing its strength by jumping on it periodically. It had to hold a body, perhaps two or three, just in case he was followed-just in case soldiers in gray uniforms thought to look for him here. He covered the roof of his shelter with mulch so that it resembled the rest of the forest floor tossing lichen, twigs and even transplanting ferns in several places.

Finished before the sun cast light into the woods, Nathan nestled safe in his dugout and fell asleep.

❖ ❖ ❖

The low beep of his watch alarm that was still set for school time woke Nathan. Once he was awake enough to remember where he was, Nathan panicked. If anything would give his hideout away, the alarm would. He turned the setting to off and took a breath to settle his pounding heart, listening. Maybe his head was ringing from so much silence, or maybe there really was a thumping sound resonating through the ground. He held his breath. The beat grew louder, mixed with breaking of brush. His eyes widened. Indeed, footsteps rattled through his chamber. How did they know he was out here? How could they find him? And so soon?

"Nate!"

Was it a trap?

"Nate, it's me, Jerry!"

Indeed he couldn't mistake Jerry's voice. Nathan pulled away the brush that concealed the entrance to his lodge and peeked his head out. Jerry rummaged through the trees. "Nathan! Where are you?"

"How did you find me?" Nathan pulled himself through the opening.

"You're here!" his friend exclaimed. "When I asked your mom where you went she mentioned the golf course and I thought where else but the old paintball field! Smart move, buddy!"

Nathan brushed the leaves from his hair as Jerry lowered a pack to the ground.

"I'm not staying long. I was just worried about you and wanted you to know I'm behind you one hundred percent. I brought you some extra food, water and comics."

"You brought comics?"

"You're going to have to do something with your time. Here..."

Jerry began unpacking but Nathan stopped him.

"Look, the idea is to stay hidden. I mean I appreciate the thought, but if anyone sees you come into these woods I'm dead meat."

"I know. I know. They won't, I promise. I've been careful and I won't come often. Maybe once a week so that you don't starve to death. I'll bring you news too. Stuff is happening that you need to know about. It's going ballistic out there."

"I only left last night."

"Yeah. One night and already they're rounding kids up and placing them."

"Placing them?"

"That's what they call it. They're putting us in jobs, or shipping us out. Someone requested me."

Nathan scowled. "Who?"

"Garcia." Jerry shrugged and handed Nathan a pile of comic books. "I'm not sure why. I report to him tomorrow. I think he would have chosen you first but your mom told the officer you were at the hospital."

"She lied for me, already?"

"Yeah, it won't be long before they catch wind. Which is why all this food. You need to stay low, Nate, really low. It's going to be too late for you to go back now. Just like it's too late for me to join you. They have a tracer on my car."

"It's here?"

"I parked at the golf course. They think I'm playing." He laughed, a grin of pride on his face. "I even brought my irons."

"Then get out on the course in case they come looking for you."

"Yeah!" Jerry shuffled the pack, not sure to leave it or throw it back over his shoulder. "Just take it." Jerry pushed the pack against Nathan's chest. "You better take care of yourself. You're the best friend I have."

"I'll think of some way to take care of all of us, Jerry. Just give me a few days."

Nathan hadn't noticed how watery Jerry's eyes were until their glances locked.

"I'm afraid, Nate."

What could he say? Those were the same words Abree spoke just before she was taken away. Who wasn't afraid anymore these days?

Jerry let go of the pack, turned and ran through the woods.

❖ ❖ ❖

Nathan stayed in the woods alone for weeks. He concealed his tracks whenever he left the dugout, and never used the trails that were frequented by locals walking their dogs, or the occasional soldier patrolling the park. Always soft footed, he only hunted at night. Necessity taught him accuracy with a slingshot, and foraging was second nature. When he was younger and in Scouts, he had learned which berries were edible and how to dig for roots he could eat. In these woods, there were enough plants to sustain him.

The hardest part of living off the land was wrestling with his conscience. He shouldn't have left his mom. She had no one. No one. Everyone in her life had deserted her and so did he. No matter how he rationalized his departure, leaving her at the mercy of an unmerciful Army tortured his mind. Was it too late to change his mind, to return to the city and enlist in the Enforcers? It'd been well over two weeks since the news of his mother's admittance into the nursing home. How long can he live like this, hiding out like a hermit in the park worrying about her?

"Nate!" Half-whisper, half-call, Nathan recognized the voice of the only person who knew his whereabouts. Though Nathan never brought Jerry all the way to the dugout in case someone might follow him, ever since that first day Jerry found him, the two would meet at the old ironwood tree.

Nathan peered through the brush. The sun had already disappeared from the horizon, leaving the faded blue light of dusk hovering over he forest. Stepping over the knotty undergrowth, he met Jerry on the trail.

"I brought you some water and some bread. Good bread not that manufactured stuff. Garcia gave it to me." Jerry pulled the commodities out of his backpack. "And candy."

Nathan laughed as Jerry tossed him the bag of sweets.

"That's the last of the candy, though. No more in the store. The Chinaman closed shop. I brought news, too. Bad news." Jerry pulled a newspaper out and then swung his pack onto his back.

"Bad news? That's the only kind of news there is anymore."

"They've got an alert out for you. You've hit the big time."

"You're kidding."

Jerry shook his head. "They want you bad, Nate." Jerry handed him a newspaper with Nathan's photo on the front page, along with the words *Wanted* in dark font across the top. When he started reading, Jerry interrupted him.

"Brace yourself before you read that. They're seeking the death penalty. Execution, bro."

"What?"

"Treason is what they're calling it, but since you left there's been other kids running off now, too. The Grays know you're influential. They want to make a public display of your demise."

Fear and adrenaline filled him. His little hideout in the woods suddenly seemed inadequate. How would he get out of this? He couldn't stay here forever. And what good would he be doing if he did? "What if I turned myself in? What would they do then?"

"I couldn't tell you. I might be able to work something out with Garcia. Maybe he can plead your case. He saved my skin. Got me a job or I'd be tilling the fields and eating that slop the Privatol spoons out. I could ask him and see what he says."

"He's one of them, Jerry. Even if he's helping you, he's only doing it because he's a nice guy, but he's still an Enforcer. He has orders and officers he answers to."

Jerry shrugged.

"No, Jerry. I've already hurt my mom. I couldn't put anyone else's life in jeopardy. It's bad enough you come here. What if they followed you? We'd both die. I'll think about turning myself in and making a deal with them, but I don't want to get you or Garcia involved."

Jerry shifted his weight and looked around the forest uneasily. "Maybe that's not the answer, Nate."

"What is, then?"

Jerry took a deep breath and looked deep into Nathan's eyes, as if ready to poor his heart out to him. "Maybe it's time for an uprising. Time to fight and die for a cause. I'm tired of being afraid and not speaking up. Where are the heroes we used to read about? Superman, Spiderman, Batman? You've held out this long. Why give in now?"

Nathan laughed at him and caught his blue eyes. "You're serious, aren't you?"

"Look, Nate. These Grays are devils. I don't want you to die in their hands. Not you or any of our friends who are high tailing it out of here. We need a plan and a leader. We need to organize and resist. Maybe confront them."

"Which of our friends left?"

"Peter Crawford's gone. I think he took off for his dad's cabin and there's rumor his father went with him. Ginny and her brother disappeared. Rumor has it they're meeting with teens from other towns and forming a resistance."

"No lie? Ginny?" Ginny was rougher than most girls in school. Some people said she did drugs, but others said she was just naturally snarky. It was no surprise that Ginny and her older brother might have ditched out of town, the free spirits that they were.

"But you're the one they want because you're like a rocket Scientist. The brainy kid with lots of charisma. You could lead an uprising easy."

"The benefits of a life of study," Nathan sneered as he read the paper that was crumbling in his sweaty hands. Who would have thought, for all he accomplished his young life, the good grades, the studying, the passion he desire he had to take care of his mom and Abree, after his mother's divorce —all that and here he is— a fugitive? All that effort and now there's a price on his head, and a bullet reserved for his heart? "I can't live in these woods forever."

"That's what I thought."

"Where are these people? The resistance? How many are there?"

"Just a handful from what I know. The Grays are on to them."

Nathan nodded, not too encouraged. "I don't know, Jerry. Maybe I should just join the Enforcers. Maybe they'd let Mom out if I did."

"Whatever you think is best, but you know releasing your mother was never part of their plan. They aren't going to let her go now. She's a mess, Nate. They've got her in a pretty bad way."

"When did you see her last?"

"I took Garcia to see his wife yesterday and your mom was there. She's wired. All sorts of sensors and feeders. They think they can read minds by draining blood, but I tell you your mom's mind is about gone. There's not much left to read."

The report sickened him. He pinched the dew from his burning eyes and looked at Jerry. "Okay, well just let me think. Let me just think about this. I'm good for now. Thanks for the candy, bro. And the water."

Jerry nodded. No more words were exchanged. Jerry ran back up the trail and Nathan took the newspaper to the dugout.

Stateside

Ivana's visit with her family had been reassuring. Glad that Papi and Auntie were healthy and safe for the time being, Ivanna felt better about returning to Sunrise. She would stay in closer contact with José, and see what she could do to help the cause. Maybe by being here she could assist her father, and save her mother and the twins from any further abuse.

Stepping out of the train station, her heart skipped a beat. A military jeep idled in the loading zone. Two soldiers watched as she strolled casually to the bus stop wheeling her suitcase behind her. She tried not to stare, but when they jumped out of their vehicle and followed her, she snickered and turned around.

Ivana inspected the starched uniforms and puffed-up arrogance of the two Grays. After her long train ride from Del Rio, she was hardly in the mood for their attitudes. Her eyes widened when the younger of the two smiled, winked at her, and spoke with a thick accent. "Ivana Garcia, we're here to show you to your new home!"

"What new home?" She squinted. "And I don't ride with strangers."

The young Gray opened the door to the jeep and nodded for her to get in. The other soldier took her suitcase from her hands and set it in the back of the vehicle. "I assure you, we aren't strangers. Not to your family anyway."

She leaned against the door and fumbled through her purse, steadying her hands less her nerves betray her. Slinging the purse strap over her shoulder she unwrapped the package of gum and offered one of the soldiers a piece. He refused. She shrugged and peeled the paper, quickly putting the gum in her mouth. "You're a stranger to me, you know. I don't take rides with strangers. How do I know who you are? You could be anyone."

The soldier laughed. "Your father's our commanding officer."

"That quick? Two months? He's a commando just like that?"

"Yes, ma'am. He wasn't offered the job on a fluke. He's an engineer."

Ivana popped her gum, all the while staring at his blue eyes and freckled face. "How did you know I was on the train?"

"There isn't anything the Grays don't know."

"Oh yeah? Then what color nail polish do I have in my purse?"

The soldier blushed.

"Yeah. That's what I thought. Why don't you tell me where my papa is and I'll take a bus to his house?"

"Buses don't go there." His smile snapped. "Get in."

Ivana pictured herself running down the street. Not her character to run, and not a good idea. Would this cocky soldier draw that gun and shoot his commando's daughter in the back? Probably. Was it worth her life to find out? She popped a bubble and cut it with her teeth, glancing at the other soldier as he positioned himself behind the wheel.

"That's what I can't stand about you guys." She slipped into the back seat. The soldier shut her door and sat in front. "Always so sure of yourselves just because you have a gun. I should have stayed in…." She didn't finish her sentence. What if they didn't know she'd been at her grandfather's farm in Mexico? Why offer the information. "I could have walked home."

They drove through her neighborhood, stopping at the corner of Pine and Ash where the Chinaman's convenience store stood abandoned, sealed with iron bars. Despite the extra security, windows had been broken; a closed sign hung at the door and it was dark inside. Ivana glanced up Pine Lane and gasped. There were no houses. None. Nathan's mom's rambler had been demolished along with all the other homes on that side of the street. The road was torn up. Bulldozers decorated the front lawns, and not a person, car, or pet was in sight.

"What the….? What did you do?" Ivana complained, not sure if she wanted the Gray to tell his version of what had happened or not.

"Progress."

"Where is everyone?" Nathan had been the one-person Ivana was really hoping to meet up with. She missed him when she was gone and never guessed that he wouldn't be here when she returned.

"They're all in their appointed places. Most of them."

The coin bank, she thought. "Testing must be completed, then?" She tried to sound nonchalant; like it didn't mean anything to her when it meant everything. Her heart beat in fear and ached at the same time.

"Yes, ma'am."

Ivana bit her lip and leaned back against the seat as the jeep rolled past her neighborhood into the hills. She didn't want to ask about Nathan or his mom. If she were going to find out where they were, she'd find out on her own, or maybe Papa would know.

They drove for a good hour, over the foothills of Sepia Mountain, through the vineyards of Greenlace Valley. Ivana knew many of the migrant workers who worked there. It was the time of year they should be in the fields, but the vineyards were abandoned. Uprooted vines were piled in rows, the ground damaged with tractor ruts and broken pipes.

"People don't drink wine anymore?" Ivana mumbled.

The Grays glanced out their windows at the landscape, but didn't answer.

"Oh. Sorry. Maybe that's classified information," she snickered.

"How long have you been gone?" the young one asked.

"Not long enough apparently."

"Too long it appears," he snapped back.

"Where the hell are you taking me?" The jeep was cramped and the bus ride from the border had been hot and dusty. She longed to take off her shoes.

Again, there was no answer. It was part of their control tactics. The less she knew of their intentions, the more power they had over her.

The jeep slowed when they approached the gated community that overlooked the valley. Once a neighborhood of wealthy vineyard keepers, Oakwood Estates was a collection of manors and small castles deemed worthy only for the elite, the rich, and now for military officers. The driver rolled down his window and scanned his ID card prompting the Iron Gate to open. Ivana watched wide eyed as they rolled past two stately homes and turned into a driveway. The Grays parked the jeep and jumped out. The driver retrieved Ivana's suitcase and the other opened her door.

"Here you go!"

Ivana followed them up cement stairs, past a row of shrubbery neatly pruned. The soldier pushed the doorbell and they waited. Ivana's attention was on the towering Tudor walls, the immaculate garden, the hedge, a drooping Japanese maple tree, and the hazy blue valley in the distance. The door opened and a servant bowed graciously. When Ivana stepped into the house, the Grays left. The servant scooted Ivana's suitcase into the hall and closed the door.

"Your father will be here to greet you in one moment," she whispered, her red cheeks blushing as she bowed, and then she too, disappeared down a hall.

The house sparkled. The hard wood floor shone like glass and smelled sweet from polish. A crystal chandelier hung over the entry and another hovered over the open living room catching rainbows that twirled on the walls. A leather couch reflected daylight beaming through the picture window. Elegant and sterile, Ivana wasn't familiar with anything in the house. There weren't even any portraits of the Garcia family gracing the hall.

"Ivana!" Her father stood at the top of the stairs, straight and tall. She hadn't seen him in his uniform before. When she left, he was still studying, still in his civilian clothes, still pondering over whether he had done the right thing. Now he looked like all the rest of the Grays. No, he looked worse. He was an officer. Fringe hung from his shoulders. A brass medal jingled over his pocket. His black leather gloves slid along the railing as he walked down the stairwell. "It's good to see you."

Ivana stepped back and chewed the tasteless gum. "Where's Mom?"

He cleared his throat. "Your mother didn't come with me. She stayed."

That didn't make sense. If Papa was a hero why wasn't mom with him? "Stayed where?"

"Home, in the neighborhood."

"What? In the ghetto they just stripped? There are no houses back there, Papa. Where did she go? What did the Grays do to her?" Her eyes scoured over his uniform. "Where are my friends? Where are the twins? What the hell are you doing?"

"I can explain."

"No. No, don't explain anything to me. You betrayed all of us and I don't really want to hear your side of the story."

He paused at the bottom of the stairwell. His eyes pleaded with her, but she refused to trust him.

"José told me something about you, but now that I see you, I don't know what to believe…."

Her father held his hand over his lips to silence her and then nodded toward a camera on the ceiling. "José the servant? Don't be silly. We don't need to talk about that now, Ivana. I thought I'd show you to your room so you can freshen up, and then we'd have a nice meal together." He offered his arm to her. She only glared at it, and then into his eyes. He smiled cordially. "Look at this place. Is this a castle or what? It's as lovely as you are."

All her questions bottlenecked inside of her as her eyes darted to the camera and back to him. Maybe it was true. Maybe Papa was a double agent and she nearly blew his cover. But if there were spies everywhere, how would she be able to have an honest conversation with him to find out?

"Where's Mama?"

He drew near. He smelled like the sickening fragrance of cologne and aftershave.

"She's in a home," he whispered. "I'm sorry. It was her choice. If she had stayed with me I could have offered her amnesty. I tried. Honestly, Ivana, it broke my heart to let her go."

"She left you? You two fought and she left? You let her go?"

"You knew it was coming."

"Why didn't you stop her?"

He shook his head, helpless, speechless. "She wouldn't…"

"I want to see her."

"You can."

"I want to find Nathan, too."

"Don't talk about that family here." It was a warning. A quiet, yet stern warning delivered with a kiss on her forehead. "Please watch what you say. Everything is recorded."

"I can't stay, Papa. I've got to get out of here. This is insane. How can I stay with you?"

"You weren't supposed to come back." He glanced at the camera.

"Is there any place we can talk?"

"Not in this house."

"Then let's get out of here. Let's go out for coffee or something. I can't breathe in here."

"My days are regimented, Ivana. I have an hour to spend with you before I go on tour." Despite the dark complexion, his cheeks were red. "I'm doing my best to keep you safe, but if you argue or go your own way, your protection is out of my hands."

Ivana tapped her foot uncontrollably, her temper brewed like a time bomb ready to go off. Her anger wasn't just at her father, but also at the forces controlling him. She shook her head, biting hard on the thin strip of gum coating her teeth.

"I don't know you." The camera couldn't hear her. The words were a steady stream of air whistling through her teeth. "This is all like alien and I'm getting the hell away from you."

"Don't…." He reached for her arm, but she slapped it away. "Don't leave here by yourself. They'll follow you. Let me call for a concierge. He can take you to where you want to go." Her father picked up the phone and pressed a button.

"Another soldier?"

"No. The servants here are civilians. Students. You might even know some of them. A few were your classmates."

Ivana folded her arms across her chest and watched her father struggle for words. Beads of sweat formed under his thick dark hair. Her brother had inherited their father's handsome features, bronze skin, and Latin nose. The two used to be so close and so much alike. "Why do you stay, Papa? Come home," she whispered.

His dark eyes planted into hers, speaking what she didn't want to hear. He had to stay. Someone had to sacrifice and he was that someone.

"Go back." He mouthed the words. All her convictions about school and politics melted away at that very moment. Papa was telling her what to do, what was important to do, and though she'd argued with him before, today wasn't the day to protest.

"Right." She wiped the moisture that was forming in the corner of her eye. "Where's Mama?"

"The Privatol Sunrise Rest Home."

"Okay. That's what I'm going to do, then. Just like you say. I'm going to go see Mama, first."

"Good."

A stiff silence followed as a young man entered the room. Jerry Carmichael. Sandy hair and pale complexion, Jerry was the star basketball player in high school. He stood a foot taller than Ivana's dad. He smiled curtly. "Ivana!"

Ivana hid her surprise, for the camera's sake.

"Jerry, take my daughter wherever she asks. She's here for a short visit and I want her to be as happy as possible. Use my van."

"The van? There aren't any seats in back of the van, sir. And it's old. Are you sure you don't want to use the limo or one of the newer sedans?"

"The van. You don't need back seats. There will only be the two of you. She knows the van. It's been our vehicle ever since she was a tot. Let her ride in it again." He smiled at her. "Maybe I'll give it to her for her birthday."

"Yes, sir."

"Papa?" She doubted she'd be back even for the night. This was probably the time to say goodbye. "Papa, give me a hug, okay?"

He embraced her and despite the stiff uniform and foreign smells, those were Papa's arms. Warm and safe. He kissed her hair. "Love you, Vana. Take care of everyone for me."

"You know I will."

Jerry shifted his weight and cleared his throat. Ivana wiped her tears and followed her escort out the door.

"Where to, Vana?"

"The nursing home." She hadn't left her suitcase in the hallway, certain she wasn't going to return. Jerry placed it in the back after she slipped into the passenger seat and buckled her seat belt. Once the engine started, Ivana breathed easier. "Is it safe to talk?"

"There aren't any devices in this van, if that's what you mean."

"What's up with everyone? What happened when I was gone?"

"Chaos. Total friggin chaos," Jerry answered candidly. "The Grays got mad because of all the resistance so they just cleaned the town out. Tore down houses, sent people away to who knows where. Enlisted some of our friends and they got their families out of the country. But some of the kids like Sam and Amy, well, let's just say you probably won't see them again. Your dad saved my hide, but my folks are gone. You're lucky, Vana. Consider it luck getting shipped out of the country. You'll go back to wherever it is, if you know what's good for you."

"We need to stop these jerks, Jerry. We can't let them take over."

Jerry laughed as he steered down the driveway. "How would we do that? It's a world Army, Vana. They don't understand American ways so they have no sympathy. They have troops Internationally, and they take more countries over by the day, enlisting their victims. Where there's one soldier, there's a thousand to replace him. You can't stop the Privatol."

"Yeah we can. A revolution. We'll find our friends and start a revolution. The word will spread. They may be a massive Army, but ordinary citizens like us still out number them."

"You're untouched, Vana. That's obvious."

"Untouched? What do you mean?"

Jerry rolled his window down and slipped his ID card into the gate. The iron bars opened. Ivana whistled. "So, they don't let you in and they don't let you out without showing your ID?"

"That's what I'm saying. They own us. And you aren't going to start a revolution because most of those ordinary citizens have already been compromised."

"What do you mean? What are you talking about? Compromised? How is anyone compromised?"

"The food, Vana. They've been manipulating personalities with the food. Your dad knows it. He doesn't eat it and he doesn't let me eat it, but anyone who does is pretty much useless in a revolution. Depending on how the Privatol plans on using someone, they feed that individual artificially manufactured food which strengthens their DNA to enhance both their physical and mental abilities and prepare them for the role. Like if they want big soldiers who are blood thirsty, they have a food that makes them that way. Or if they want someone smart there's a special food for that. Or if they just want them complacent so that they do what their told, they've manufactured a food for that."

"Get out of here!"

"The NCF. Newly Constructed Food. That's what it is, Vana. The Grays have been plotting this for years. They're controlling the genetic makeup of every person in every one of the countries they've conquered, and soon the whole human race will be at their disposal."

"How do you know this?'

"Your dad and I have talks. He knows."

"Then Papi wasn't just telling me a fairy tale?"

"It's the truth. There might have been a time I would have questioned it, but I've seen the transformation in our friends. Remember Ricky Hanyard? The little guy that liked to garden?"

"Yeah, I remember him."

"Remember how short he was?"

"He was puny, yeah?"

"Ricky enlisted. When the Grays asked him what department he wanted to serve, he answered that he wanted to be in combat."

"No lie?"

"He's six feet tall now. His hands are as big as a dinner plate. He's a guard at the rest home."

"No way. How did that happen?"

"It's the food, Vana. They can feed you to be anything. Smart, big, complacent...."

"Stupid?" She snickered and looked out window. "Why don't people just buy their own food and to hell with the Grays?"

"Haven't you noticed? Or haven't you been here long enough? You see any stores open anymore?"

"No." It was true. The shopping malls and grocery stores on the way to her father's house were boarded up. The market places closed and some had even been bulldozed. "I knew they were doing something with the food, but not to this extent...."

Jerry snickered. "We aren't allowed to have any commerce. That gives them control of everything we eat. That's how they keep down the revolution. They can make you into anything they want with their gray mash."

"Creepy." Ivana's stomach turned.

"Creepy and real."

"So how do you get around it?"

"One down side to what they're doing is that the crops they grow don't reproduce. They must keep the good seed. Your dad's job is inspector and he tours the labs, the facilities where they grow NCF's. He's got a key to the storehouses underground and he brings us real grain before they process it. It's not much, but it's real. He's got all sorts of recipes he's given the cook. But if anyone finds out, he's a dead man."

"The red ant."

"What?"

"It's a story Papi told me before I left. Something about ants and the Quetzalcoatl. He called Papa a red ant." There had to be more to the story. It wasn't like Papa to steal just to save himself and his servants. José said he was smuggling seed to the farm, but if Jerry knew about the smuggling, he hadn't mentioned it so she kept silent.

"You want me to take you to the nursing home?"

"To see Mama, yeah, and I want to find Nathan."

Jerry snickered again. "Nathan Barber?"

"What of it?"

"He's an outlaw now, you know? Got his mom in big time trouble they say."

"Nathan wouldn't get his mom in trouble."

"He did. He's hiding out. They'll shoot him if they see him, and anyone with him."

"How do you know that?"

"It's in the papers. Mrs. Barber's being watched like a hawk. Cameras all over the woman."

"How do you know?"

He turned to her, his smile contorted into a disdainful scowl. "Ivana, maybe my folks aren't in that home, but everyone we know knows someone in there. Rumor gets around. Molly Barber is a cooked crow!"

"That's awful."

"It's true. The Grays are certain someone's going to be coming around looking for Nathan and will approach her about her son. You go see your mom, but you stay away from Molly Barber."

"So where is Nathan?"

"You think I know?" Jerry's face turned red and he looked in his rear-view mirror, bit his lip and tossed his hair as he changed lanes.

"Do you?"

"I'm not saying. Not even to you."

Ivana crossed her arms, watching traffic as they sped down the freeway. The barren landscape whizzed by. Ivana rolled her window down but hot air and dust filled the already roasting van. Either that or suffocate, she thought. Finally, Jerry brought the van into the city. They waited at a light.

He tapped the steering wheel, glancing anxiously out the window. "You are the only person in the world he'd want to know his whereabouts."

"Then tell me!"

Jerry shook his head. "Go visit your mom and then let's get out of town. Where are you going? Back to Mexico?"

"Where is Nathan?"

He stopped talking as they approached the barbed wire fences. Ivana recognized the home as the same facility where the students were tested. Now the whole complex had been made into a rest home. "This is it? This is the nursing home?"

"This is it, Ivana. This is where they take anyone they think they can't use anymore. They feed them brain mash." He nodded toward a group of guards jogging. "You see them?"

Ivana watched the troops running along the dusty street, their boots hitting the ground in rhythm to their grunts. They were all big men, uniform in size. Other sentries stood by the double doors to the facility, rifles resting on their shoulders. "I see them. Why?"

"These guys get fed the same mash as Ricky. Pig mash"

Ivana stared. "What?"

"Look at them. You see those guys running over there? The Grays are breeding them to have an endless appetite, making their bodies so big and strong that they become killing machines. Remember how they used to give hormones and steroids to athletes back in the day? Same thing here only this stuff works on your brain too. Your dad says it's from pig DNA.

He's knows what he's talking about. Tread lightly, Vana."

"I just want to see Mama. I promise I won't eat anything."

Jerry grabbed her arm before she opened the door. "They'll ask for your ID. Use this." He handed her a card stamped with a military clearance. Her image, an old photo her father must have had stashed away for a day like this, was on the inside, sealed in a thick plastic sleeve.

"Thanks."

When she stepped out, Jerry parked the van. Ivana tried not to stare at the soldiers. Unable to control her pulse, she took charge of her stride instead, and walked casually to the double doors of the nursing home.

Two guards met her, big men filling their uniforms. Their size didn't bother Ivana. She'd seen big men before although these soldiers were at least a foot taller than her. What bothered her were the glazed eyes and large fingers that hovered over the trigger of their semi-automatic weapons. A captain approached just as Jerry jogged up to Ivana and stood beside her.

"Pass?" the man asked, his accent thicker than the young soldier Ivana had been with that afternoon.

"Two passes here, sir. Ivana Garcia, the commander's daughter is here to visit her mother."

The man laughed and brushed the passes aside. "Go on. Be quick. They go to bed at dusk."

"Yes, sir." Jerry took Ivana's arm and ushered her inside.

"You're coming with me? I thought you were just going to wait outside."

"Believe me; you don't want to do this alone."

It was a good thing Jerry came. Foul smells churned her stomach the instant she stepped inside the building. Had it been smells common to nursing homes, she could have handled it. But there was another odor, the smell of death. She clung tighter to Jerry's hand as he led her through the long hallway, past the room she recognized as the testing room, no longer furnished with desks and tests papers. They stepped into a courtyard and entered an adjacent building that reeked the sterile smells of a hospital.

"May I help you?" a woman asked from behind a desk after they stepped through the double glass doors.

"Maria Garcia, please." With a trembling hand, Ivana handed the nurse her ID card.

"Daughter?"

"Yes."

"Are you staying with your father, Commander Jacques Garcia?" The woman was scrolling through her mother's files on the computer.

"I…." She glanced at Jerry. His eyes warned her. "Yes."

"I see. Let me trace her. Yes, she's in the dining hall right now. Up the elevator and down the hall to your right. You can't miss it."

"Thanks."

"Wait. We'll need you both to wear these." She took Ivana's hand and clipped on a small bracelet. A red light flashed in the center. "No one comes in here without a tracer. Sorry for the inconvenience."

Ivana watched wide eyed as the woman slipped a bracelet onto Jerry.

"Security," she smiled.

"Right."

How strange this all was. Her father a spy, her mother incarcerated in a horror house. Only a year ago she was on the Sunrise High Debate team, her mom had just come back from a tour of France and Dad had been promoted to chief engineer at CMB. Now she rode a cold and sterile elevater to a third story floor where her mom was kept prisoner, and her dad had to work under cover to keep his family alive.

When steel doors glided open Ivana stepped into a well lit dinning hall. small tables were uniformally arranged, with one person seated at each table. Ivana immediately recognized her mother. Surprisingly, she was in a wheel chair. Her mother had never been in a wheel chair before. There was nothing wrong with her. Ivana had expected a warm greeting from her, or perhaps a cheerful embrace, but the woman only gave Ivana a blank stare when she walked up to her.

"Mama. It's me. Ivana!"

"Ivana?" the woman repeated as though trying to remember.

Ivana sat across from her, glancing briefly at the plate of food her mother had been eating. A pile of gray porridge sent a stream of steam into the air carrying the nutty fragrance of grain. Ivana glanced up at Jerry and he nodded. This was the food he had told her about.

"Mom, you need to get out of here." She pushed the food aside. Her mother pulled the plate back. Ivana leaned close to her ear and whispered. "Don't eat the food. It's bad for you! C'mon. Let's go to Papa's and I'll feed you something good!"

Her mother laughed, spitting the remains of what was in her mouth, she coughed and then laughed again. Her eyes welled with tears as the hysteria continued. Ivana sat upright.

"I'm serious, Mom. Let's go back to Papa." Ivana glanced around the room expecting the residents to be staring, but they weren't. Perhaps they were too drugged to mind the commotion. Only a few nurses looked their way and one of them walked toward her.

"You are funny, young lady. Very funny," her mother said, fanning her now rosy cheeks.

"I'm not trying to be funny. I'm trying to take you home."

Her mother shook her head, wiped her mouth, and locked eyes with Ivana. "I will never live with that man again. No. You know what your father is. He's not my husband. This is my home. This is where I belong. And the food tastes good."

"Excuse me, miss. It's bed time for our patients now." The nurse rolled Ivana's mother's chair away from the table.

Boiling with anger but unable to release it, Ivana nodded to Jerry. "Let's get out of here." She couldn't leave fast enough, and yet making a scene would be disastrous. On their way out, Ivana caught sight of another woman being wheeled through the hall. If the middle-aged blond hadn't been so heavily guarded with medics, Ivana may not have noticed her. The spider web of tubes, and the flashing lighted bracelet drew her attention.

Molly Barber! Nathan's mom. Ivana stared, and Molly looked up at her. Whether the woman recognized her or not, Ivana couldn't tell, but the grief in the woman's eyes was more than Ivana could bear. Jerry tugged at her arm.

"Let's go."

❖ ❖ ❖

"What a horrid place. I can't believe it. Mama all messed up like that. What did they do to her? Why?" She held back the tears. "All her life she lived good Jerry, and to end up like that. I can't stand it. Damn Grays! And Molly?" She looked at Jerry, but he kept his eyes on the road. "A fishnet of tubes. Did you see Molly Barber's face? I'll be damned if they do that to my mom."

Jerry remained silent. Streetlights came on as the sky faded. A sudden urge to be back in Mexico dug at Ivana's heart. "Why did I even come back here?" she whispered as Jerry took an unexpected turn on Oakland Boulevard.

"Maybe there's something you have to do." Jerry spoke softly.

Ivana knew this road well. They were nowhere near the highway, nor were there any junctions from here that lead to one. This was a back street that bordered the golf course and ended at the park. Jerry was up to something and Ivana could only hope she knew what he was doing. Once past the greens, the van curved around switchbacks until they passed the county marker. He pulled into a parking space and stopped.

"What kind of shoes do you have on?" he asked.

"Sneakers."

"Then you won't mind doing some hiking?"

They exchanged a knowing glance and Ivana's heart raced. She threw open the door and jumped out as Jerry took a cautious look at the parking lot and the road that led to it. Without a word, he led her into the shadows of the woods. Ivana didn't dare ask him where they were going. She knew.

There were no stars out. The sky was beyond sunset, but too young for moonlight. Ivana's night vision soon guided her on the narrow trails until they were deep into the woods. When they came to a large ironwood tree, Jerry stopped and cupped his hands over his mouth, hooting the sound of an owl. They listened to silence. He called again and the sound echoed from somewhere distant.

"Step lightly and try not to break any branches." Jerry walked through the brush, away from the main trail. Ivana followed ducking under the low growing limbs that ripped at her hair. When they came to an old gray stump hidden in a thicket of mesquite Jerry stopped. Ivana held her breath, waiting, listening. The rustle of twigs underfoot announced that something or someone approached.

"Ivana!"

The sound of Nathan's voice sent shivers up her spine. His dirty face and matted hair, shirt tattered and crusty blue jeans were not typical of the Nathan Barber she remembered, but his smile was the same and it tickled her. She hugged him, and he squeezed her tight. He smelled of earth and sweat, and his warmth was comforting.

"What the hell are you doing out here?" she asked as she peeled away from his embrace.

"Hiding."

"Why? What did you do?"

"Nothing. That's just it. They wanted me to join the Enforcers and instead I bailed. I made them mad, I guess, so they put a warrant out for my arrest."

"Nathan aced the tests, Ivana," Jerry explained. "They wanted him as an officer in training and figured they could use his influence to bring our friends around. With Nathan refusing their offer, they lost ground in our neighborhood. And the fact that close to a month has passed without finding him, they're putting the pressure on. They've been asking his friends to turn him in, offering a bounty and amnesty. Heck, they came to me, but with your dad as my boss they backed off quick. They're threatening to kill

Nathan if they catch him on the run."

"Oh, my God! Nate!"

Nathan shrugged. "I'm trying to devise a plan, here but…." Nathan's eyes widened as he gazed over Ivana's shoulder. Ivana couldn't see what he did, but she saw a flash on the branches above them. Nathan grabbed her wrist and pulled her into the brush, pushing her low to the ground. She crawled behind him silently in the dirt, and gasped when she slid into a deep hole. Jerry jumped into the trees opposite them.

Nathan pulled a limb over the dugout and sunk into the shadows.

"Jerry?" Ivana mouthed and then held her breath when she saw a ray of light bouncing on the surface. She curled up against the damp wall and listened.

"You there! Come out into the light. Who are you with?"

Jerry stuttered. "I'm alone. I swear!"

"No, you are not. Who is with you?"

Ivana recognized that voice, the thick accent of the young Gray that had given her a ride to her father's house. The soldiers must have been watching every move she made that afternoon.

"It's just me. No one else."

"If that's the case, then what are 'just you' doing out past curfew?" the soldier sneered.

"I was on my way back home when the engine on the van started giving me trouble. Kept stalling. You know anything about engines?"

"Your engine stalled?" The soldier laughed. "So, you walked into the forest?"

"I had to pee."

"Where is your passenger?"

"What? What passenger?"

"The girl. Ivana Garcia. The one you were with."

"She…I left her at the home, with her mother."

"All right! I think we need to bring you back to where mama is, and question you there, eh? Henrich, handcuff him and put him in the jeep.

We'll go see if this girl is indeed with her mother. If not, I say we let him visit the old woman instead. Maybe they could have dinner together, eh?" He laughed again, an evil laugh that burned Ivana's insides.

"You'll have to answer to Commander Garcia for this!" Jerry protested.

"I answer to Commander Garcia for everything. I think he will be interested in learning that his van is on a desert hillside with his daughter's suitcase in it, and no daughter. I think he'll be offering a reward for the kidnapper of his daughter. I don't imagine you know who it might be though, do you? Let's go."

"Let me stop them," Ivana whispered and moved toward the entry, but Nathan held her back and shook his head. He covered his lips with his finger. They waited until the beam of light ceased to bounce off the trees, and the sound of footsteps tapered into the distance.

"I could've just popped up there and told them everything was cool."

"You think? It's past curfew and no one comes up here at night. They'd arrest you as quick as they arrested him. Why do you think they were following you?"

She paused to reflect and realized she was indeed a suspect to Nathan's whereabouts. "They think I'm going to lead them to you?"

He nodded. "Wait here." Nathan crawled out of the dugout and Ivana prayed. She heard the motor of the jeep as it drove away, and Nathan's feet as he returned.

"We have to save him."

Ivana took his arm and climbed out of the hole, brushing twigs and dirt off her clothes. "They said they were going to take him to where your mom is. Where is that?" Nathan asked, breathless.

"They're heading for the retirement home, the same barracks where they tested us."

"Was Jerry lying about the van?"

"The van is fine but I don't have a key."

"That's your dad's old van, isn't it?"

"Yes, why?"

"I can hot wire it. What about your father? Do you think he'd just call the guards off? After all, Jerry is his employee, and you aren't kidnapped. Surely you could think up a story to tell your father."

"Papa's out of town. He left right after I did."

"I wonder what would happen if you just walked in there and used your father's authority…."

"I can do that. Just get the van started and I'll be on my way."

"I'm going with you?"

"That's insane. What if they see you?"

"What if they don't believe you?"

The intensity in Nathan's eyes drilled hers. "If the Gray's think you and Jerry are up to something, they'll do everything to get a confession out of you. If you want I could turn myself in."

"No! They'll kill you. We'll go together and rescue Jerry and get out of town. I'll drive because they'll be looking for this van."

"Fair enough."

After hotwiring the car, Nathan slid into the back.

Serum

Sterilize the needle, find the germination pods, insert needle and press the serum into each little pocket. Easy. Tedious. The first day Abree worked with Jaden and it was a pleasure. They talked, and teased and once he pretended he shot himself and had her laughing. But the trainer walked by the window and they had to act serious, and get back to task. That might have been the reason that Abree was by herself the second day.

By the third hour she was bored, thankful the buzzer finally sounded for lunch. She rinsed the needle and took it apart, taking each component and setting it in the sterilization compound, took off her latex gloves, dropped them in the slot for garbage, and left the room. The halls were empty by the time she headed for the elevator, but her legs were tired and hurrying just wasn't in her.

When she passed the dark rooms, she stopped. Even though she wasn't supposed to know what was in there, she did. The animals that were bound tight in cages could be heard crying if she listened. Temptation to open one of those doors and release them all gnawed at her. That'd be heroic. And stupid.

Abree stepped into the elevator alone. Being so new to this place, it was easy to get confused. Her mind was on lunch, and she wasn't completely awake. She accidentally hit the wrong key on the door and instead of stopping on the main floor, she ended up on a lower level. Unaware that she wasn't anywhere near the dining area, she stepped out and walked through the hallway. It wasn't until the first junction where the tiled walls turned to earth that she realized she had made a mistake.

"Oh man! I messed up! How could I be so stupid?" The walls smelled damp, musty, and like a basement. Clearly this wing was not taken care of like the rooms upstairs. In a way, the earthen halls offered comfort. Especially when she saw a row of ants crawling along the floor.

"Makia, did you do that?" she laughed to herself.

Several kernels of corn bounced above the red ants as they shuffled the seed along the assembly line. Abree followed the formation until she came to a room —the door to which was ajar.

She paused before she stepped inside. No one was in the halls so she let her curiosity lead her over the threshold. Amazed with what she saw, she gasped.

This was the storehouse of good seed. Rows and rows of jars hung from their lids attached to shelves. Each jar labeled with code and descriptions. Each jar filled with corn seed. Awed by the discovery, Abree walked through the aisles, reading labels. Seed from the Southwest, red, blue, Zuni, Hopi. Seed from Europe, and Scandinavian countries. Seed with catchy names and different colors. Large and small. Seed from the mid-west, sweet corn, field grain. There were varieties of every color and geographical location. "How many kinds of corn could there be?" she whispered.

"An infinite number," came an answer she did not expect.

She froze. On the other side of the cluster of jars stood a man in a lab coat with a sanitation mask on. He stared her.

Abree's heart jumped to her throat. "I...."

"Abree Barber!" the man said, his voice slightly above a whisper. He took his mask off to reveal a handsome smile. His dark eyes twinkled. "What a pleasure to find you alive and well."

"Mr. Garcia? What are you doing here?"

He laughed. "I'm afraid I need to ask you the same question. This entire floor is off limits. I'm assuming from your attire that you are a Lab?"

"Am I in trouble?"

Mr. Garcia glanced out the window, a seriousness swept across his face. "I'm afraid if we're caught down here we'll both be in trouble."

Abree turned to shut the door, but he stopped her. "No. It will set off the alarm."

"I should leave."

"Wait. Please. This is no small coincidence, the two of us meeting like this."

"Why is that?"

He signaled her toward the back of the room, into the shadows and away from the door. "Things have happened at home with your family. Bad things."

"What happened?"

He knelt in front of her, his hands on her shoulders, struggling to tell her something. "The Grays took your house, and your mom is living in a…a home. Your brother is wanted. He's in a lot of trouble."

"Why?" Stunned at the news, she held her breath, waiting to hear more.

"He refused to do what the Grays wanted him to do. Abree, listen to me. I want to save him, and you, and Ivana."

Abree scowled, not sure of his intentions. "Why are you telling me?"

"Because you can help me."

"How?"

"Don't say a word that you saw me here, not in this room. If you see me some other place, don't let on that you know me. And don't eat the food. I will send something to you when I can. What's your number?"

"O67."

"Okay, I'll make sure I get you something wholesome to eat."

It seemed odd, Mr. Garcia telling her these things, but she nodded. He patted her on the arm and stood. As he did, Abree saw the pocket in his coat bulge, lumpy like it had corn in it. "Good. Now, find the elevator and go upstairs. Not a word."

She nodded again and ran out the door, not once looking back.

One Good Thing

Ivana rolled down her window at the nursing home and flashed her ID in front of the sentry.

"State your affairs."

"I'm on my Papa's business this time, soldier." She popped her gum. He was a Native. One of the Grays who had most likely been recruited from her hometown, snatched out of the National Guard, maybe because he was a big guy, or maybe because he liked to eat gray mash. Whatever the reason, Ivana read the word 'traitor' on his forehead.

"Get to it then, ma'am."

She stepped on the gas, drove the van to the entrance and parked.

She pulled her purse off the passenger seat, glancing into the back of the van as she did. "Ready?"

Ivana's strut through the courtyard to the nursing home was nothing less than seductive. Glad the Accent-Boy wasn't on duty today, or that he was perhaps looking for some kidnapper in the forest outside of town, she smiled at the sentry, stepped through the door, and found the nurse at the desk congenial.

"Are you here to visit your mom, again?" The woman studied her computer. "Maria Garcia and you are…let's see. Ivana! I remembered!"

"Good job! But I'm not here to visit. I'm here to take Mom home."

"I beg your pardon?"

"Papa sent me here to get her. He wants to take care of her at home.

He says she'll do much better in that big old house on the hill and I think he's right, don't you?"

"Regardless of where she'll have the best care, I'm not sure I have authority to release her to you."

"Excuse me? Isn't my father the commander of this compound?"

"Well, yes, but...."

"Then wouldn't his word be law?"

"We'd need more than just a statement from his daughter to act on that request. We'd need something in writing."

"Fine." Ivana pulled an envelope from her purse and handed it to the woman. After a moment of reading, the nurse looked up at Ivana.

"I'm sorry. I'll have to get this approved."

Ivana shrugged and the woman slipped into the office, closing the door behind her. Ivana reached over the desk and pushed the tracer button on the computer. A list of names appeared and she scrolled through them, highlighting Jerry Carmichael. Room 4, lower level, only a few steps from the front desk.

When a young man in uniform entered through the glass doors, Ivana held four fingers up to him. He turned down the hall and Ivana deleted the search just as the woman returned.

"I'm sorry Miss Garcia. Policy is that your father will have to come here himself. We just can't release her to you."

"Oh, no!" Ivana pouted and took back the paper, folded it neatly and returned it to her purse. "I'm devastated. I was looking forward to spending the afternoon with Mama, on the porch at Papa's house. Can't I just bring her home for the day?"

"I'm sorry. The best we can do is have you visit her here."

"Well, where exactly is she?"

"Just a moment and I'll trace her."

Ivana shifted her weight, unwrapped a stick of gum and bit into it, tossing her hair over her shoulder.

"Your mother is sleeping right now. You can wait...."

The soldier came back through the hall, escorting Jerry through the front door.

"Look, that's okay. I'm going to come back when Papa gets home. Let her rest."

Ivana backed away through the exit, arriving at the van just as the soldier and Jerry shut the door behind them. Ivana jumped into the front seat, stepped on the gas and drove through the gate.

Once on the highway, she burst out laughing. Nathan pulled his hat off and unbuttoned the uniform coat.

"Man alive! I didn't think you'd pull that off, Nate!" Jerry laughed.

Nathan cut the band to Jerry's tracer and reached for a screwdriver in the toolbox, unloosing the wires to deactivate the sensor. "Best thing about this jail break is I got to take a shower at Commander Garcia's house."

"As much as I hate the Grays, you look hot in that uniform," Ivana said. "Nice of Papa to lend you one!"

"Where are we going, Vana?" Jerry asked.

"Mexico." Ivana and Nathan both chorused.

The Race for Dinner

Abree arranged the yellow plates of food on her tray just as she always had and carried it to the table. She glanced at Jaden. He ate gingerly. The Gray's must have control of the poor boy's mind by now, what with the candy that he eats, and the piles of mash that he devours. How could they not?

Jaden looked at her. "What? Sit down. Eat. All this work makes me hungry. Doesn't it you?"

Abree shook her head. If anything, the work made her sick to her stomach.

"What's wrong with you, O67?"

She frowned. "Don't call me that. You're my friend!"

"But even friends have their boundaries. I really think you need to chill more than you do. It's time to smell the roses so to speak."

"There are no roses here, Jaden."

"There are all sorts of roses here. We're so fortunate, you don't even know. Look at this place. Secure, warm, untouched by the weather."

"I wish it were raining."

He snickered. "You have a bad attitude."

"Yes. And it's getting worse."

"Why?" He dabbed his mouth with his napkin and took a drink.

"Because I'm losing the only friend I had."

"Correction. Two friends. You had two friends," Jaden reminded her.

"Makia's gone." Abree pouted.

"But where? Do you know?"

She didn't. Abree had no idea where Makia was, but she hoped beyond all reason that she would see him again. "I'm going to my cell. I don't feel well."

"You need a Hall Monitor to get to your room," he reminded her without even looking at her, as though he wasn't concerned about her well-being any more.

"I'll find Nam." Abree had never left the lunchroom without Jaden. Still, with all the warnings about not eating the food, watching Jaden devour his lunch the way he did made her tremble. She didn't want him to succumb to the Grays, but it didn't appear as though there was a way to stop him.

"Nam's gone." Jaden gave her a matter of fact look and continued chewing.

"What?"

"They promoted him. He's not in charge of our hall anymore. We have a new monitor now. Over there." He pointed with his eyes. Brian Gallard stood by the door in his white space suit uniform, chest puffed out like he owned the lunchroom, taser on his belt, hands folded across his chest. Abree groaned. What worse thing could happen?

"Would you like me to tell him you're sick?"

"No." Abree sat next to Jaden, catching his wry smile. "Shut up!"

"If I were you, I'd stay away from your cell as much as possible. He's already been over zealous with the Labs. I saw him zap two of the workers this morning just for being slow."

"Great."

"Like I say Abree, just join the program. There's no sense in fighting because you aren't going to win."

Abree's stomach turned as she watched Jaden eat. She was famished, but too afraid to touch the food despite Jaden's encouragement.

"Why do you eat it if you know what it does to you? It's like giving in. Like you have no hope."

"I have no hope. I'm like you, Abree. What this Privatol is doing is tragically wrong. I think this whole business of manipulating everyone's food for the sake of eugenics is wrong. But I'm tired. I don't want to fight. I want to find some way to just be happy, and if not happy, then content. If this food is designed to take the stress away, then it will make my life easier."

"That really disappoints me."

"Why?"

"Because I thought maybe we could find a way to get out of here, or to stop what the Privatol is doing, or to at least let the animals out of their cages, but you're giving up."

Jaden shrugged, but he kept eating. "I'm hungry."

Abree left when he did, slipping the unfinished dinner into the trash as indiscreetly as she could. Jaden saw her, but he wasn't a snitch even if he did sympathize with the enemy.

When evening came, she walked with Jaden to his cell, wished him a good night, and then hurried to her own. Brian was there. He bowed cordially as he opened her door. "At your service, Miss!" he said, his face blushing red from bending low.

"What's with the bow?"

"I'm just showing off, letting you know how well I have it and you don't."

"Good grief."

"I don't get locked up in a cage like some people I know. Just want you to remember that, and to know who's boss around here."

"Boss? Whatever."

"Ha! You'll say whatever when I exercise my authority!" He fingered the buttons on his waist just as Abree stepped into the cell. "I'll be back in half an hour."

"Half an hour?"

"Yes ma'am. Inspection. The Commander of Operations will be here tonight and everyone gets up and shows him their brilliance! When I open your door, you stand outside by it. Your bed will be made, your suit hung in its proper place, and a salute until he says at ease."

"Okey dokey!' Abree gave him a sneer and in return he zapped her with a tinge of electricity on her cheek. "Ow!" She held her hand over the wound. "What did you do that for?"

"Talk to me with respect, Lab. I insist on it. Say it! Say 'yes sir'."

She glared at him.

"Say it!"

"Gallard!" Nam was in the hall, jogging toward them, his voice excited. "You have authority to use that thing when the Labs act up, but you aren't authorized to provoke them. Do you know the difference, or do you need to go back into training?"

"She was being disrespectful."

"I heard everything. You were in the wrong and I don't want to see it happen again."

"Yes, sir."

"Now get down the hall and get ready for Inspection. Look sharp. And grown up if it's possible."

Brian gave Abree a dirty look and then pivoted around, stalking away in a huff.

"Are you all right?" Nam touched Abree's cheek where the electric charge had burned her. "It's red, a little blister, but it will heal. Stay out of his way."

"Thanks for rescuing me."

"Well, he is one of my charges. If he looks bad, I look bad. But I don't want to see you get bullied, either. You're too good a worker."

"Thanks."

"Everyone's a bit nervous about tonight. We haven't had an inspection in a long time. I don't ever remember one. But Commander Garcia, the bigwig from uptown will be here with a couple of his officers. Man, I hope we pass."

Commander Garcia? She grinned.

"Into your cell with you. Your door will open automatically when he comes to this wing."

"Yes. Sir." Abree smiled. It was nice having Nam on her side.

The door closed and Abree sat on her bed, not sure what she should do. Half an hour was not enough time to sleep though she was certainly tired. She rested her head on her pillow, and when she did, she felt something unusual, a pouch about the size of the palm of her hand. It was filled with something. She reached in the bag and pulled out a handful of meal. Cornbread? Oh, my gosh. Mr. Garcia promised he would send her something to eat. Hunger winning any reservations she had, Abree ate the entire loaf in a matter of minutes, savoring even the tiniest of crumbs that fell from the bag. Her head fell against her pillow when she was done, her tummy full, and her heart thankful. Tears of gratitude rolled down the side of her face, and though she shouldn't have, she fell asleep.

The sound of her door opening woke her up. Light glared into her room. Footsteps alerted her to someone marching down the hall. She heard both Nam and Brian's voice shouting orders.

"Rise up! Inspection! Hup to!"

Abree jumped out of bed and stood next to her door, surprised to see so many cells on her aisle opened with children standing next to them; children she hadn't even known existed. Abree tucked her stomach in and stood straight. Brian barged into her room, and Nam followed. Commander Garcia and the three officers stood at the door.

"What is this doing here, Lab?" Brian held up the bag that the cornbread had been in, swinging it in the air for all to see. "Look at this!" he shouted. Nam gave Abree an accusing stare as the officers stepped into her cell.

"You are out of line, O67, and you will be disciplined," the tallest of the officers said. His white suit was starched and so bright that Abree had to squint to look at him. Brian smirked.

Abree froze. She hadn't had time to hide the pouch, and now her crime lay open to not only the people who ran the facility, but the commanding officer as well, the officer that gave her that bread. Her eyes met Commander

Garcia's. Indeed, he was hiding his guilt like a champion. He didn't speak. He didn't say one word. What did she expect him to do? Admit he had snuck it into her room? Or was this a trap to get her in trouble?

The other officers looked at him. Commander Garcia took the bag from Brian.

"I'm sure there's an explanation. No need to be so hard on the young lady."

"We have policy here, sir. There are no outside belongings allowed in any of these quarters." The tall officer grabbed Abree's arm, the other unfastened his handcuffs from his belt.

"Well, then we'll just take it away." Commander Garcia rolled the pouch up and put it in his pocket. Brian's mouth hung open, but he didn't speak. Nam gave Abree a daggered look.

"At ease, gentleman. Don't handcuff the girl. No one is in trouble over this. I'm sure it's just a misunderstanding. How long have you been here, Miss....?"

"Abree...." She almost said her last name and then remembered the warning Mr. Garcia had given about her brother, she hesitated.

"Well, we'll be more careful about having items such as this in our rooms from now on, won't we?"

She scowled, not sure why he winked. "Yes, sir. Sorry, sir."

"Carry on!" Nam signaled Brian to move down the hall. Commander Garcia followed the others, but not without giving Abree a nod.

She watched him as he moved from room to room, a general disinterest in inspecting anything, but more concerned with making eye contact with the children. He was so different, so real. Just watching him made her homesick for her family. More than that, it gave her hope.

Once the inspection was over and the men had moved on to another wing, Abree returned inside her cell, but the door didn't close. Instead Teacher Francis appeared.

"Get up."

"Why?"

"Discipline."

"But the commanding officer said I wasn't in trouble."

"Did he?" The woman pulled her handcuffs from her belt and locked Abree's wrists behind her back. "Well perhaps he didn't want to make a public display. He saved your face. But he did call for you in his office and I don't expect it's for cake and ice cream."

With a shove, the woman pushed Abree down the hall to an elevator. They ascended more floors than Abree knew were in the facility and when the elevator door opened, Abree saw the night sky for the first time in months. Huge domed windows covered these halls and the air was fresh, as though she was breathing real oxygen. Teacher Francis guided her to an office, rang the buzzer and waited for the door to open. A Gray let Abree inside and dismissed the Teacher.

Before the soldier could announce Abree's presence, the commander stepped into the waiting room.

"Dismissed soldier. I can take it from here." When they were alone, Commander Garcia shut the door quietly. "Abree, come into my office, please."

Commander Garcia's office not only had a large oak desk, but he had cupboards, a refrigerator, and a sink along the wall. There was a window behind the commander's desk and it was open. Through it Abree could see a million stars, a hazy horizon and the distant hills. She breathed in the fresh desert air. She had already come to trust Mr. Garcia, yet when he pulled a key from his desk drawer and unlocked the cuffs, she trembled.

"Are you all right?"

She nodded.

"Care for some hot cocoa?" He smiled as he poured hot water from his carafe, spooned out some cocoa from a canister and sprinkled a bit of sugar into the cup. "Please, sit down."

Abree fell into the easy chair, rubbing her wrist. Mr. Garcia set the cocoa in front of her. The aroma was so pleasing she smelled the steam a few times before she took a sip.

"We have a problem."

Abree's eyes widened.

"Because that monitor-boy made such a big ordeal about the pouch…." the commander shook his head, "the pouch I gave you…all eyes are on me right now. I can't risk being scrutinized. I'm forced to do something about this infraction. I want you to know that my decisions are based not only around your well-being, but around the work that I'm doing."

Abree wasn't sure how to respond. She nodded and then shook her head. She had no idea what Commander Garcia was trying to say.

"Well, I'm going to be honest with you. Like I told you before, I can use your help. This uniform, it isn't me."

"You're not a Gray?"

"I am. I mean I've enlisted and I'm a commanding officer, but my heart is not with them. I'm secretly working for the Resistance."

"There's a Resistance?"

He laughed. "Of course, there is. You can't oppress as many people as the Privatol has without a Resistance."

"Well, where are they? Are they doing any good? Because I'd sure like to get out of here."

"I realize that and I'm about to help you get out of here. In answer to your question about where they are, the Resistance is underground. Literally."

"How literally?"

"You remember where you met me, in the stock room? There are tunnels to that room. Many of these tunnels are connected to other storage spaces, other seed caches under different facilities."

"And what does the Resistance do in these tunnels?"

"Smuggle good seed to farms that can grow it. The Privatol has confiscated nearly all unadulterated seed in America and they are using it to create their artificial crops. Those crops they raise are scientifically designed to alter a person's physical and mental make -up depending on what sort of DNA is introduced into the plant's cells. That's been your job, Abree. That's what you've been doing in the lab."

"I thought it was probably something evil like that."

"Evil. Yes. They can take a person's blood and determine exactly what kind of protein they need to add to it to alter that person's behavior and physical appearance. They formulate their crops accordingly. It's an ingenious way to manipulate humans."

"And why are you telling me? Isn't it pretty dangerous to know all this?"

"Yes, but you're already in danger, Abree. They know the level of your intelligence and they have little patience. Without you cooperating with them, you risk an even worse fate."

"Like what?"

"They have the science to take your blood and read it, as if reading data from a computer. They can then do anything they want with that information. They can transfer it to others, or simply store it. It would leave you a vegetable." His eyes became teary as he spoke. "I've seen it happen. I don't want it to happen to you, or to any of the children in this ward. I need your help."

"You think we can stop them?"

"I'm not sure if we can stop the movement of this political order, but I think we can prevent them from manipulating the entire human race by keeping a steady supply of untainted seed available to the farmers who are protected. At least, that's my mission."

"Protected? Who protects them?"

"There are vigilantes surrounding our farms that keep them safe."

"Okay, so what do you want me to do?"

"As I told you, in your situation I need to make a decision. There are people I must answer to. They didn't like the leniency I showed you earlier. I have to accommodate their wishes so that I can continue my mission without being a suspect."

Abree felt feverish. "What are you going to do to me?"

"The most merciful thing I can do is ship you out of here."

"Where to?"

"We have a compound nearer to the border. It's not like this. It's more of a prison."

Abree bit her tongue. How could this nice man stand there and tell her he was going to send her to prison? Her fists clenched, but before she could burst out of the room he touched her shoulder.

"It's not what you think," he whispered in her ear. "Your friend Makia is there and he's working with us."

Abree's eyes grew wide. "Makia is there?"

"He's a runner. These facilities are connected and he's one of the people that transport. Most of the soldiers at the facility are of the Resistance. You won't know whom at first, but they'll identify themselves to you once they know that I sent you there. After that, you'll be treated well. It's actually a lot safer for you there than it is here."

"One thing." She hoped Mr. Garcia would honor her request, but she was a little hesitant to ask.

"What's that?"

"Can you send Jaden there too?"

The commander was silent for a while. He ran his finger over the grain of the desk, a contemplative scowl on his face. "I will give it some thought. That's the best I can tell you. I don't know Jaden well enough yet. It would of course, depend on his chemistry."

"What do you mean?"

"I mean, if he's been eating much of the food, his mind may already be taken, which would mean he'd be impossible to work with. We've discovered that there's a threshold. Once past that point, allegiance to the Grays is unshakeable.

"He's not a snitch. Honest."

Commander Garcia smiled as he stood with the handcuffs. "I respect your feelings toward this young man. I cannot however, promise anything. Now if you would, please?" He nodded toward her hands. "We have to do this for show."

Abree reached out her hands and let him cuff her. He called the guard, whispered something in the man's ear, and slipped back into his office. Abree was escorted away as a prisoner.

A Chase

The van kicked up desert dust as it raced through the night. The conversation had lulled. Jerry had fallen asleep and Nathan sat up front, nodding out.

Ivana yawned. It had been a long drive, the day stressful, and she couldn't remember when she slept last.

"Need me to drive for a while? You've been at the wheel all night." Nathan rolled down his window after catching Ivana's yawn.

"Maybe. We can't cross at the border with you looking like that, though. You know? That uniform won't work."

"What do you mean? I can fake an accent."

"And get gunned down as soon as you hit town?" She snickered. "I don't know Nate. Sometimes you don't always think things through."

"Seriously, Vana? Get gunned down?"

"Okay, so you've never been to Mexico, and that gives you an excuse for being ignorant, but yeah. That's what José says. He says the gangs in Del Rio shoot Grays."

"No lie? Well, I have my tee shirt in my pack."

"Then the Americans will discover your identity. I think we need to take the river road and find another way to get across the border."

Ivana turned east at the junction, fighting heavy eyelids. All she really wanted to do was find some place to pull over and go to sleep.

"Border patrol," Jerry announced, his nose peeled to the back window.

"Where?" Ivana glanced in the rearview mirror.

"On the side of the road. Didn't you see him back there?"

123

"Where? That car we just passed?" She looked over her shoulder and saw a pair of headlight in the distance.

"That's the one!"

The river basin was a haven for border patrol searching for illegal immigrants or drug traffickers. Since the Grays took over, border laws had become even harsher than ever, disallowing anyone from crossing into Mexico except at certain checkpoints and then only American citizens who had amnesty cards would be allowed to leave the US.

"Man, he just pulled out!" Jerry's breath fogged the window.

"Crap!" Ivana's grasp tightened around the steering wheel. She tossed her hair out of her face and breathed deeply, but that didn't work. Her nerves were shattering. "Get down, Nate. Hide or something. Jerry, get your face away from the window!"

"Hide where?" Nathan slid into the back next to Jerry. "There's nowhere to hide, Vana."

"Okay, okay. Keep calm. Nate, grab a piece of gum out of my purse." The van swerved when she reached back, her hand grabbing for air. Nathan found the gum, unwrapped a stick and placed it in her hand. "Holy Mother, get us out of here!"

"Just drive normal, Vana." Jerry peeked out the back window again.

The lights maintained a steady speed behind them.

"He's going to stop us. I know he is."

"Don't think negative, Vana. He's probably just going home."

"You think? A lone vehicle out in the desert at three in the morning headed for the border and he's going to just let us go? I have a feeling. I just know it. Like psyche, you know? Kind of like tarot cards or something. I feel it coming. Ever have that feeling?" Neither Nathan or Jerry responded. "Well, whatever it is, I've got it."

"Get rid of it. Try to think positive." Nathan sounded like a schoolteacher. Ivana glanced back at him. "Get down."

The headlights grew brighter.

"No. He's going to stop us. You two need to disappear. And hide that uniform. We're better off as civilians right now. Isn't there a blanket back there?"

"No blanket, Vana."

"There's a space blanket in the wheel well. I'm sure of it. Papa always kept emergency supplies in the wheel well."

She heard them shuffling about in the back. "Well?"

"Yeah, we got it. It's under control. Just drive straight."

Lights filled the van as the trooper's car closed in. Ivana's heart leapt to her throat when red and blue flashers invaded their vehicle. A siren sounded. Ivana pulled over and rolled down her window, but she didn't turn the engine off. She dared not glance behind her for fear she'd give away her friends' camouflage. Every movement she made could be used against her. She bit into her gum and tried to calm her racing heartbeat.

The flashlight blinded her when the trooper came to the window.

"Hands above your head," he ordered. Ivana obeyed. "You alone?"

"Yes, sir."

The light rolled over her eyes again, into the front seat and then toward the back, though it couldn't stretch around the corner to reveal the occupants. Ivana held her breath.

"What are you doing out here on this lonely road at this hour?"

"Going home, sir." Ivana hoped the tremor in her voice wasn't noticeable.

"Is that right? Where's home?"

"It's down that way. Along the river. My grandfather's place."

"You have ID?"

"Yes, sir." She reached for her purse and pulled out the ID that her father had made.

"Papers on the van?"

To her relief, the papers were in the glove box.

"I know pretty much everyone who lives down that way. No Garcias that I'm aware of."

Maybe he was baiting her to talk. Ivana said nothing.

"All right. I'm going to follow you and make sure you arrive safely. A lot of crime goes on out here. The border is no place for a pretty young girl like you driving around at three in the morning."

Ivana popped her gum and looked at the man. "I'm used to the rough neighborhood. I can handle myself."

He returned her papers. "You're not going to change my mind, Miss."

She made a point of looking cool when she shoved the papers back in the glove box. She had to slam it shut twice to make it stick. The trooper turned off his flashlight and got in his car. Ivana pulled away before he started his engine.

"I should have driven," Nathan mumbled, his head buried in a shopping bag.

"You'd be on your way to your execution if you did. I'll get us out of this."

"Just step on the gas, Vana," Jerry urged. "Just high tail it down the road. He's only a lone ranger. He can't get you."

"What? An old Dodge van against a Camaro?"

"That's not a Camaro, Vana. It's a Dodge Charger. And you've got all-wheel drive. Take her cross country."

"You're a whacko, Jerry!" No way was she going to try and out run the trooper. She had to think though, and fast. The hot air that blew in the window took a dip in temperature as they neared the river. She turned left off the highway that paralleled the river and would have eventually brought them to the border crossing an hour a way. Cottonwood trees hovered over the road, which turned to gravel, and then graded dirt. Her insides shook, the rear-view mirror jiggled, and CDs fell from the visor.

Ivana slowed. The trooper's headlights proceeded at a turtle's crawl, headlamps flickering as he trailed behind over the bumpy terrain. Fences appeared, and driveways concealed by low growing, thick and snarly mesquite trees.

"Okay. You guys are going to have to think smart. I'm going to choose one of these driveways, park and go into the house. When I do, you're going to have to somehow abandon ship because the cop is going to shine a flashlight in here and you are dead meat if he finds you."

"What? Are you, insane?" Nathan asked. "You can't walk into someone's house at three-thirty in the morning."

"I can't?" Ivana popped her gum, turned the van around 180 degrees and backed it up a driveway, shining her lights in the trooper's car. When she killed the engine, she could hear the trooper's radio mix with sounds of crickets and bullfrogs and a rushing Rio Grande. Dogs joined in the chorus from every house in the neighborhood. Ivana looked in the mirror, fixed her hair, and applied a layer of lipstick.

"Good God!" Nathan mumbled.

"Shut up. You'll be thanking me for this. If you noticed, I put your door away from the house facing those weeds. You can dodge out as soon as I make enough noise to get this trooper dude's attention."

She didn't hesitate to swing her legs out of the van and slide off her seat. She waved at the trooper and then walked to his window. "Thanks for the escort, man. I appreciate it."

"I'll leave when you're safe inside."

"Right, well could you at least dim your headlights? My grandpa's kind of old and doesn't like getting woken up."

"I can do that." The lights dimmed. Ivana peeked at the van from the corner of her eye, noticing Jerry's foot emerging.

"Okay. Well, I need to find my keys. Could you shine your flashlight here in my purse?"

The trooper laughed and obliged as Ivana rummaged through her purse. "Man!" She pulled out her gum and offered a piece to the trooper as Nathan and Jerry dodged into the brush. Close the door she thought. Oh, good God, close the door.

He shook his head. "No thanks. We aren't allowed."

"How stupid of me. Of course, you aren't. Hang on. I think I put my keys in this side pocket. Yep! Here they are!"

"Do you want me to walk you to the door?"

Ivana glanced at the van. Someone was running back into the woods. Nathan had returned to shut the door. Good! "Well, I don't know. It's just over there. No sense upsetting the pit bull." She grinned. "Grandpa keeps him in the house. He's well mannered, but he doesn't really like uniforms. Or men. And sometimes he slips by me when I come in at night. It's a bear getting him back inside, especially if he's, you know, feeling predatory."

The man's eyes twinkled. He could just be humoring her. Heck for all she knew this was his house.

"So anyway, thanks for the police escort and I'll see you later."

Ivana took her time walking to the porch. By the sound of the police radio the trooper was either running a scan on her car, or a warrant check on her. When she got to the steps, the light came on and her heart stopped, but she kept walking. There was no need to touch the doorknob, it opened and Ivana's mouth with it.

A middle-aged woman peeked through the crack. "Can I help you?"

"Mama!" Ivana said, pushing first her foot and then her torso through the crack. "You waited up for me."

"I don't know you. Who are you?" The woman jumped back in horror, her eyes wide. Ivana slammed the door shut and put her finger over her mouth.

"Shh."

"I'll hush you!" A book flew past Ivana's head.

"No please, don't. I'm not here to hurt you. I'm not! Honest! I'm just…well I'm running from that man out there."

"What man? Is this some kind of scam?"

"No! This is not a scam. Look. He's a state trooper." Ivana pointed out the window. There was no mistaking his police car. And yes, the trooper was searching the van, shining his flashlight into the windows.

"Oh, my Lord! Who are you? Are you an escaped convict?"

"No, but I have two people with me who are wanted by the Grays."

"Oh." The woman relaxed and stood straight, pushing her short-matted hair out of her eyes. "Well, that changes things. I understand. You've come to the right neighborhood. There's not a man, woman, or child here that can stand the Grays. When that trooper leaves, we'll get your friends inside and clean them up. The gall of them! Chasing young people around like they do, arresting them, and putting them in prison camps. Are you from Silver City?"

"Sunrise."

"Oh my dear! A crying shame how they tore that city up. I feel for you, honey. Here, go hide in the bedroom. If he comes to the door I'll just tell him you're my daughter. A sorry world we live in when we trust the convicts before we trust the law." The woman hustled Ivana through the hall and into a small but neatly kept bedroom, switching on a lamp as she did. "Make yourself at home. My name is Melinda, but like I say if that man comes to the door I'm Mom. We'll look for your friends when he's gone. Where're you headed?"

"My grandpa's farm in Mexico. We'll be safe there. We just don't know how to get across the border."

"Don't worry about that. My brother lives just up the river and has a barge he uses for things like this. He's a soft heart for young people, too. We'll get you all straightened up. This can be your room. You kids stay here until you've got some meat on your bones. Some real food! Not that plastic stuff they feed you up north."

"Man, I appreciate this!" Ivana couldn't remember when she felt as safe. "We can't stay though. The sooner we cross the border, the better off we'll be."

"All right. Have it your way. No one's going to keep you prisoner here. Good heavens you've had enough of that, I'm sure!"

The bed was wrapped tight with a hunter green spread, the posts and backboard a dark ebony. There were no decorations aside from several photographs that hung on the wall and an antique alarm clock on a shelf under the window. The policeman's headlights still beamed through the curtains, but they dimmed and the patrol car soon backed out of the driveway. Melinda sighed when the taillights turned back up the river road and disappeared.

Ivana fell back on the bed in relief that her pulse was finally normal. After a few minutes, Melinda came back with a flashlight.

"Come on. Let's find your friends. There's a loft in the den where they can rest while I call my brother. There should be enough time for you to take a nap before he gets here. He'll help you get to where you need to go."

Prison

At least they gave Abree back her t-shirt and jeans with the rhinestones on them. She was wise enough to have stuffed the bandana Nathan had given her in the pocket, and for that she was very thankful. She hadn't seen her possessions for the entire time she was at the Lab, supposing that they had been thrown out, just like her suitcase had been tossed into the dumpster. She was certain she'd have to change into prison clothes again, but at least she had a reprieve from the space suit.

As she waited to get "checked in" she could see the inmates moving about in the plastic cubicle behind the desk. They wore green jump suits. Not a dull green like the janitors at her school used to wear, but a bright lively green, so bright they probably shone in the dark. Abree's mom always said she looked good in green. Had to do with the red highlights in her hair, and her complexion.

"Abree Barber," the woman behind the desk fidgeted with her a starched collar. No one else was in the room save for the officer who had transporter her here, a young woman with a stiff jaw and beady eyes that refused to look at Abree. Granted it had been a long and grueling ride in the hot desert, but the officer could have at least joined in a conversation.

Abree walked up to the desk, unassisted.

"You will be in cell 67." The woman smiled. Abree sneered. How convenient she gets the same room number as her lab number.

"Officer Jenkins will take you there."

The young woman who had brought her saluted. The security door buzzed open and Abree walked into the prison. Immediately the cool of an air conditioner hit her. Almost too cool, she shivered. Her eyes scanned every room they walked by. First, she saw a gym where both men and women exercised, doing pushups and running laps. Abree was never very athletic. Hopefully they wouldn't make her do push-ups. She hated push-ups. They made her stomach hurt and she couldn't really do them right anyway.

Officer Jenkins turned down another hall that passed a dining room where all sorts of sweet smells met her. "I wonder if they serve real food," Abree whispered.

"I beg your pardon?" Jenkins turned to her with a complacent stare.

"Never mind," Abree answered. What with that expression, she didn't really need an answer. Officer Jenkins was as Gray as they came.

Further down the hall were cells that had doors adorned with bold black numbers. Unlike the sealed cells of the facility she came from—where one couldn't even tell where the obsidian wall opened—these were ordinary rooms. Midway through the hall they came to room "67."

"This is it." Jenkins unlocked the door and opened it, ushering Abree inside. There was nothing in the room that spoke prison. The bed had a bright pink comforter draped over it and piles of quilt covered pillows. A fridge, lamp, and a desk furnished the room, and behind the long lacy curtains was a window. A window! Abree pushed the curtain aside to look out over the miles and miles of golden desert, and in the distance a ribbon of green along the horizon.

"Is that the Rio Grande?" Abree turned to Jenkins.

"It is." The young woman set the key to Abree's room on the dresser. "Don't lose this. It's very difficult to have another one issued."

"You're giving me the key to my room?"

"Why wouldn't I?"

"Well, it just seems odd. Not that I mind. So, what do I do here?"

"Whatever you want except escape. If you try to escape they'll either shoot you or send you somewhere else."

"Whatever I want? That seems odd."

The girl shrugged. "There's a schedule in the desk drawer that tells you the regimen. Breakfast at 8, work out at 10. You can go into the courtyard between noon and three, after lunch. There's a pool, a hot tub, and a tennis court. Whatever you want to do during the day. If you want to write a letter, mail pickup is at 2 and you have to take your letter to the front desk to have it stamped."

"That's amazing. I thought we were prisoners."

Jenkins stared at her for a bit, her green eyes glassed over, as though she didn't really see Abree. Finally, she cleared her throat and said, "We are."

The door shut and the officer was gone, leaving Abree scratching her head.

No one had asked her to change her clothes, but because she had worn her jeans all day in the jeep she wasn't against the idea. Abree rolled open the closet door in hopes of a wardrobe, prison garb or not it didn't matter. Several bright green uniforms swung from their hangers, clean and smelling fresh like they'd just been ironed. "They actually look kind of comfortable. A shower and some clean clothes and then a walk through the 'prison'. Maybe I can find Makia."

❖ ❖ ❖

Late afternoon turned the sky pink. Abree had been to every corner of the facility yet she didn't find anyone who knew Makia or knew of his whereabouts. At least no one that would tell her. Discouraged, she stood on the porch outside the exercise room—a long cement veranda two stories above the ground overlooking the pool and hot tub. Beyond the prison's walls, the desert view stretched out before her.

Several crows called from their perch on the fence as though announcing the evening. Odd creatures they were —too large to be called birds—Abree was never very fond of crows. Before the days of takover, in Sunrise the crows would hover over her mom's garden in the back yard as if waiting for the corn to ripen and then laughed when they raided her crop. Corn. Odd that she should think of corn at a time like this.

Abree turned to see a man in uniform watching her, but when their eyes met he walked away. Curious, Abree followed cautiously until he stepped into the elevator, the light indicating he was descending. To what level she didn't know, and she didn't know if she should pursue him, or just go to bed. Her curiosity, and her determination to find Makia and help the resistance prodded her to step in the other elevator and hit the ground level button. This prison wasn't like the lab, and the elevator seemed much safer. Why, she wasn't sure. Was it because of Commander Garcia's promise that she'd be treated better?

The door opened to low ceiling halls and a damp musty smell that was all too familiar — the smell of tunnels. When Abree turned the corner, she paused only long enough to notice the same man disappear into the shadows. She hurried after him.

"What are you doing here?"

Abree jumped at the voice that spoke from the depths of the dark hallway. Her hand raced to her chest as her heart beat against it.

"How did you get here?" Makia asked.

"Oh, Makia I've been so worried about you."

"And I you."

"Commander…."

"Shh." He cut her off and grabbed her arm, leading her back to the elevators. "It's not safe to talk here."

Makia took Abree to level one, hurried her through the lobby, and into the courtyard. He slowed once on a narrow flagstone trail bordered with cacti and sagebrush. The color of the fading day illuminated the gold of the ground and turned the whole world into a shimmering jewel. The call of a mourning dove broke the stillness. Makia veered from the path up another dusty trail which skirted the side of a hill well hidden from prison walls and which overlooked miles of desert sands. Cottonwood trees marked the path of the meandering river.

"Now we can talk." Makia sat in the dirt and patted the ground as a request for her to sit with him. "Did Commander Garcia send you here?"

"He did." She dusted her jumpsuit and sat next to Makia. "I take it he sent you here as well. That was your discipline?"

Makia nodded. "He's a good man." His eyes searched hers before he spoke. "Did he ask you to help him?"

"Yes. He didn't explain very much, but he asked me to help. I'm on your side, Makia. I just need to know what to do."

The boy's eyes fell back to the sunset. Brilliant colors of turquoise, pink, and gold illuminated the earth. "He's taking a big risk. Bigger than any risk that you and I will be taking. His heart is gold. He is saving so many people."

"I know."

"I'm not sure how long he will be safe. Do you remember what I told you? About the ant people?"

"I do. And after we talked I saw the ants in my cell stealing a grain of corn."

He smiled.

"And I said to the walls just like I'm talking to you, 'What do you want me to do, Makia? Learn from them?' Like you thought I should steal corn?"

Makia laughed and she joined in. "Stealing corn! That's what the ants were doing? I think they were telling you something. But Abree, it isn't stealing. The Great Spirit gave us life and with it we were given a planting stick to till the ground, but these Gray-clothed people have robbed us of the seed. Our seed. They replaced it with corruption. With evil."

"The ants were telling me something, weren't they?"

"The ants see a kernel of corn and they take it. They don't know ownership, not for food. They come and take what they know will nourish them."

Abree watched the sun set on the horizon—as if it were sinking into the Cottonwoods to bathe in the cool Rio Grande. The moment captured her attention and she chuckled at the thought of the sun taking a bath in a river. In that instant she knew life would be good again. Hope had returned to her. "Makia, how did your people start talking about the ants? Where did that legend come from?"

Makia drew his breath. "Well…." He shifted in the dust, stretched, and then began his story. "We believe that before we came to North America, our people lived in a city that is no longer in existence."

"Where?"

"South of here. South of Mexico."

"Mayan, maybe?"

He shrugged. "Maybe. Our ancestors lived so simply that the creatures of the Earth loved them. When the floods came, the ant people taught our ancestors to survive by breathing through reeds while under water."

"Wow, seriously? That is awesome. I mean, if it really happened."

Makia turned sharply. "Of course, it happened."

"It's amazing that a tribe living in the middle of the desert would have a legend about a flood. Breathing through reeds is kind of like snorkeling, isn't it? Only I don't suppose your people have ever done that?"

Makia shrugged. "It's amazing because it's true. When you are one with life, it all makes sense."

"I'm different than you, Makia. I never really spent much time thinking about nature. I love walking in the park. And I love animals. Pets mostly. I always wanted to have a horse someday. But I like my technology, too. I like to play games."

Makia nodded, but he didn't seem to agree. That was just a difference they'd have to live with.

"I'm glad you came here. I was worried about you." He gave her a shy smile.

"Me? Thanks." Abree blushed, but the seriousness in Makia's countenance remained.

"I had a vision when I was still in the confines of that cell." He shuddered at the thought and then fell silent.

"Tell me."

"I saw a Kachina."

"A Kachina? What's a Kachina?"

"Kachinas are the spirit of different life forms in this world--the spirit of the deer, the sun, the hunter, and many more. There are way too many to name. In our ceremonies, the men of the village dress as the Kachinas and dance, giving homage and respect to those forces of the world, but the Kachina in my dream wasn't a man dressed up in ceremonial garb, like at our dances. This one was real."

"What spirit was he?"

"I don't know. He was like a dragon, but with feathers. I'm not sure what his name is. I've never seen him before. Maybe the elders have. He scared me when I saw him. His face was frightening. What was even scarier was that he talked to me."

"What did he say?"

"He said to feed the black ant people," Makia scratched his head. "I don't know what that means." His hair shimmered when he shook his head. "It was just a dream. Maybe it didn't mean anything."

"Maybe. What did he look like?"

The brilliance of the sun had already fallen past the horizon. Reds and pinks shimmered on the few clouds that reflected its light, back-dropped by turquoise turning to purple. "Like that." Makia nodded toward the sky. "His colors were the color of the sunset, and his face...." His voice tapered to silence and Abree gasped.

She saw it too. The face of a dragon, flaming red eyes and turquoise feathers danced across the sky.

Without warning, Makia jumped up and took her hand. "Come. We have work to do."

"Where are we going?"She stood, but his haste confused her.

"To the tunnels."

"Stop!" Abree froze, her hand locked in his, and she pulled him back. "I don't know this place. I don't know anyone here. I mean, who are the good guys and who are the bad guys? I have no idea what to watch out for! If I go to the tunnels I need to know who my enemies are. I don't want to get caught."

"They didn't tell you?"

"No! Who didn't tell me? The only thing I got from anyone here is that the guards are prisoners too."

Makia grimaced and studied her. "Who told you that?"

"Officer Jenkins."

"Oh. Well yes, we all know who Officer Jenkins is. She told you she was a prisoner?"

"In so many words."

Makia nodded. "I think she has eaten too much of the gray food and it's taken its effect on her. The Commander thought he could save her, but he has since said he believes it's too late, that she's crossed the threshold. The prison she speaks of is, no doubt, her mind."

Abree stared at him, thinking on his words, and of the Commander's concern for Jaden. Not once had she ever considered what would ultimately happen to people if they kept eating the fabricated food. Her own experience had been scary enough. For others who didn't have a chance to come out of it, they were wholly transformed. Monsters even. Some strong, some smart, and most were fed into not caring about life at all. Like how Jaden was becoming. How long could anyone consume the gray food before it made them nothing more than a vegetable, or a killing machine? "What's going to happen to Jaden?"

Makia shrugged. "Maybe the Grays will let him go. Maybe he'll come here."

"I don't think so. Commander didn't seem to want to release him. I think it's because Jaden was ...well, the last time I talked to him he was giving in. He wanted me to give in, too. I don't think he's going to make it."

She knew there wasn't anything Makia could say, and she was glad he didn't try. His words would have been wasted. She didn't want sympathy. She wanted her friend. It was sorrow she saw in Makia's eyes.

"There are too many people being destroyed: people like your friend Jaden. We've got to run with the seed. If we don't save our food, then someday there will be nothing safe to eat. Run with me. Think of your friend. Think of your family."

She didn't need Makia to convince her. She had come to the prison willingly, and with anticipation of joining the Resistance. Questions that bothered her would be answered in time. She would learn who the enemy was, and who to trust. Makia would help her to know. "Let's go!"

The Resistance

The halls in this basement were not as developed as those in the basement of the lab. The storerooms lacked lighting and they were much larger. Rows upon rows of containers stretched into the depths of the underground cache, and Abree wondered if indeed there was an end to them.

"Who labeled all these?"

"Different people. I don't know. They were here when I got here." Makia was articulate about which jars he would open, gather seed into his pouch, and then close. After each handful of seed, he tied the bag with a string to keep it separate from the next. Abree followed him, watching both what Makia was doing and keeping an eye on the door, which they had left slightly ajar.

When Makia's bags were filled, he handed Abree a pouch and began pouring seed into it.

"Hurry, Makia. I'm getting a creepy feeling," she whispered.

"Shh."

"Like I think I hear footsteps. Listen."

Indeed, the muted sound of boot heels on dirt came from the hallway. Makia and Abree ducked low in the shadows and against a table. Abree could see the crack of the entrance and a gray uniformed figure approach. She saw a hand touch the doorknob to close it, but they hesitated.

"What do you see, soldier?" An accent. Abree held her breath. The ones with the accents were the worse.

Makia's eyes were wide. He stooped, motionless.

"The seed room has been compromised, sir." Officer Jenkins responded.

"So, it has. Who keeps the key to this room?"

"I believe, Sir, that the only key is kept in the Commander's office, sir." Her voice was flat and complacent.

"That's what I thought. Well, the evidence is mounting, isn't it, Officer Jenkins?"

There was a pause in their conversation. Abree wondered why they weren't entering the storeroom. Surely, they suspected someone was in here. As much as she didn't want to be caught, it seemed strange they would speculate a break-in and not investigate. The reference to the Commander sparked a new fear.

"What should we do, Sir?"

The door creaked open wider and the sunburnt face of a well decorated officer peeked into the room.

"We will ask questions, Jenkins. We will ask many questions." With that he stepped away, and the two left.

Abree exhaled, her heart still racing. They waited a good while before Makia zipped open his jumpsuit and tied the pouches around his waist. He took hers as well, and hid them inside his coveralls. "I'm running. There's a rendezvous at four. I'm sure it's almost four now and it will take ten minutes to get there. You don't have to come with me. You should go upstairs and act like you know nothing."

"I can't leave you."

"What will you do?" His whisper was angry and sounded like a cat hissing at her. "It's too dangerous now. I'll do this alone."

"I'm in this with you. I can be an extra set of eyes and ears. I'm not going upstairs by myself!"

With no time to argue, Makia jumped up, and raced out the door, Abree at his heels. They ran. Away from the elevators, away from the storage rooms, away from any light into dark foreboding tunnels, a hollow vein under the earth. Abree panted; her chest hurt from lack of oxygen, and her knees were becoming numb. "Stop," she pleaded. "Can't we walk from here?"

Makia's breath was as short as hers. He nodded and waited. "We're almost there."

"How can you tell?"

"The air gets cooler. There's another tunnel that joins this one, the river air comes through it. Feel it?"

Abree could tell the difference in temperature now that Makia had mentioned it. The air was fresher too, and more pleasant to breathe.

"I hear them."

There were voices coming from the junction. Makia took a step in that direction when a flash of light beamed behind him. A loud pop and a shrill whistle sent him running to the wall. Fire and smoke and a round of gunfire came from the adjoining tunnel, returned by another volley of gunshots behind them. Makia grabbed Abree's arm and dragged her around a bend where they took cover and watched the gunfight pursue.

The men Makia had come to meet had machine guns. They took turns stepping out and firing their rounds. Sulfur filled Abree's lungs. Still, she held in her cough for fear of drawing attention. The Grays had only handguns, but they dodged bullets by hiding behind the tunnel beams. They aimed carefully.

Machine guns rattled again. A Gray was hit. Someone shouted in a foreign language and then soldiers hauled the wounded man back the way they had come.

Once the Grays disappeared, a blanket of silence fell. The tunnel fell into darkness again as the only flashlights had been the ones the Grays had carried. Makia and Abree's jumpsuits had a glow of their own, but at this moment, nothing shone.

Abree could hear breathing.

"Kid! You there?"

"Wait here," Makia whispered to Abree, still trembling. He unzipped his jumpsuit and unfastened the bags, throwing them over his shoulder before he closed his suit. "I'm here."

"Kid! You okay?"

"Yes."

Makia stumbled when he pulled away from the wall. He had been shaken from the fight, but he was brave and Abree was proud of him as his faint profile moved toward the men.

"Lay low for a few days man," one of the men said. "They're wise to us. You don't want to be the one they nail."

"No sir," Makia said, dropping the bags in the dirt. "I'm going to hide out a little while before I go back."

"You do that. You wouldn't want those Grays seeing you pop up. I'm sure they have a bullet or two left."

"Yes, sir."

Makia moved away from the men, toward Abree. She didn't want the strangers to see her. Even though these men were running the seed to Mexico, still they had machine guns and they were frightening. Abree hugged the walls of the tunnel and stood perfectly still until Makia walked by. He took her hand as he passed and pulled her deeper into the darkness. Not a word was spoken until they were far away from the junction and the men had left.

"I don't see how we can go back upstairs now with the Grays down here. Maybe they followed us!" Abree said.

"We can't, now. We'll wait. There are not many Grays against us in the facility. Once our friends find out what happened, they'll get us back in."

"Will they find us all the way back here?"

Makia was quiet for a moment. "No. We'll need to go nearer to the elevators."

Abree hesitated to walk back down the tunnel where the Gray had been shot. "There might be more soldiers waiting for us. Maybe they left a scout or two down here to lurk in the shadows and ambush us."

"Maybe," Makia agreed. "Maybe not, though."

Her confidence returned to her once they cleared the junction. It was too dark to see anything so if Abree couldn't see well enough to spot someone, then the Grays wouldn't be able to see either. Not at least until they were close enough to put up a struggle. She giggled picturing her and Makia jumping on a Gray and beating him with their fists.

"It's really hopeless, you know," Abree laughed.

"What is?"

"Us taking on the Army, the world power. We aren't going to get very far."

"Not alone, we won't, but didn't you see the dragon in the sky?"

Abree bit her lip. How vivid that image had been. "What does a dragon have to do with this?"

"I don't know, except that it told me to find the ant people. That's all I know."

"Okay. Then who are the ant people? You know I'm not going to believe you if you tell me there are ants walking around underground, and talking and having a merry old time stealing corn." She had a sneer on her face, but when Makia looked at her she wondered. "What?"

"What did you just say?"

"I said I wouldn't believe you."

"No. What did you say about the ant people? That they were walking around and what?"

"Talking. Stealing...."

"Don't you see it? That's us. We're the ant people."

"That's absurd. Why would a dragon tell you to be like yourself?"

Makia's eyes widened. "Why would a dragon tell me to be like myself? Who else would I be like?"

"Now you're just playing with words." He was such a tease, except when she considered his eyes, he wasn't teasing.

"Just be real, Abree. That's all life wants from us."

❖ ❖ ❖

They waited by the elevator for a very long time. No one came for them. Abree's stomach growled and her eyes grew heavy. "I don't want to wait any longer."

Makia yawned. "Then let's go. I'm ready for bed."

Maybe she should have been more suspicious when she stepped into the cage and hit the button, but weariness had gotten the better of them. It wasn't until a flash hit their eyes did they realize the security cameras had been activated.

"Don't say a word," Makia whispered. "Not one word."

"Well you just did."

What difference did it make now if she spoke or not? They were caught coming up the elevator from the storehouse floor. The Grays knew someone was in the seed room. Who else would it have been? Surely the soldiers found their way down to the junction by following them. Makia was lucky it wasn't his back that stopped a bullet. Still, for Makia's sake she wouldn't talk. She couldn't think of any lies to tell when they asked her, but she wouldn't say anything to hurt Makia.

The elevator opened normally. The halls were empty. Abree said goodnight to Makia and walked to room 67. When she opened the door, her bed was made, and on it was a note.

"Dear Abree

They are calling me in for questioning.
Please contact my daughter in Mexico.
Thank you for everything.
Garcia."

"Oh no!"

Plea for Seed

I'm just asking for a moment to think, Ivana," Nathan argued. Melinda and her brother stood by the door waiting for Ivana and Nathan to come to an agreement, but Nathan wasn't going to consent to leaving so soon so easily. He had just crawled out of the woods with Jerry after having ridden in the back of a van all day. They'd been running like scared chickens ever since Jerry got caught in the woods.

"People always escape in the dark, Nate. That's the way it's done." Ivana popped her gum.

"Would you stop that?"

"What? Stop what?"

"Popping your gum." He glared at her. She looked away. "Okay, look. Let's wait till dawn. Is that possible?" He looked at Melinda, who nodded hesitantly. Her brother shifted his weight, so Nathan addressed him. "Is that okay with you? If we do this after we get some sleep?"

"I can't sleep," Ivana interrupted. "If the cops come they'll see us crossing the river if we wait until daylight."

"Who's going to see us in the middle of the river? And if someone does see us, who is going to know it's us? And even if they know it's us, who's going to stop us? I mean this is the Rio Grande! It's not like they're going to drive their cars into the river after us."

"They'll shoot."

"It's not that I don't appreciate your help," Nathan addressed Melinda and her burly brother. Melinda had introduced him as Jake, the Riverman. "And we do need your assistance getting across. I'm just not so

146

sure we should be rushing off at night. Isn't it kind of dangerous? I mean we'd be risking your life as well as ours."

Jake shrugged. "Do it all the time cat fishing."

"C'mon Nate," Ivana pleaded, badgering him for consent.

Nathan glanced at his friend, but Jerry was no help. His head fell over his chest as he napped.

"Thing is, you're dealing with the border patrol on this river come morning. I'm not so sure I want to wait till then. Don't know what'll happen if they catch me smuggling kids across the border. Whatever the costs, I can't afford it."

Ivana crossed her arms. "See?"

"It's your barge." Nathan stood and shook Jerry awake. "Let's go, chum."

"What? Now? Why can't we wait until morning?" Jerry blinked the sleep from his eyes.

Nathan pulled him up by the shirtsleeve and the four walked to Jake's truck. Ivana took shotgun and Nathan and Jerry jumped in the back. Jake threw a tarp at them. "Cover up with this. They know me around here, but they don't usually see me transporting teenagers. Never liked them much before. I'm the one that complains about the parties you folks throw. Scare the fish away!"

Nathan slid under the tarp and huddled next to Jerry, who had already fallen back asleep.

❖ ❖ ❖

The truck stopped near a shallow beach where Jake's barge was tied half out of the water. No one spoke as they embarked the rickety barge. Nathan had his doubts about its safety. The dark river gushed along, a threatening void daring the little band of refugees to confront it. The sound of rushing water, and the swift-moving current nudged him into reality. He could drown in this river.

Once they stepped onto the barge and seated themselves on the splintery wooden benches, Jake picked up his long oar and pushed the raft away from shore. Within seconds they caught the current, rotated in circles, and floated quickly down the river.

Nathan hadn't suspected he'd be crossing over to Mexico by way of the Rio Grande in the deep hour of night, riding rapids and hanging on for dear life. Jake's barge was nothing more than a raft with sides in which their bodies could easily spill over. He glanced up to see if Ivana and Jerry's knuckles were as white as his.

"What's the matter kids, catfish got your tongues?" Jake laughed as he pushed the boat away from a rock with his oar. He guided the barge like a kid does a skateboard, bouncing over the whitewater and twisting around boulders with a steadfast smile that shone in the moonlight.

"What's there to say?" Ivana had great control over her voice, but her teeth clamped together after she'd spoken.

Jerry's eyes were glued to the bottom of the raft.

One last surge and the barge hovered over calmer, deeper waters, and then drifted with the current to Mexico.

"You've done this before?" Nathan asked after he finally exhaled and the man steered them to a sandy beach.

"Wouldn't be right for me to say— being as anyone crossing this way usually does so without the government's approval."

"We'll never tell!" Jerry jumped from the barge, tripping over the rail and landing hands first in the sand.

"Hey, if I can swing it I'll get you some money for this sometime," Ivana said. "Honest. I'll remember you folks."

"Yeah. Just go on and stay out of harm's way." Jake was already backing the barge away from shore. "Get! That's the Coast Guard now!"

Nathan didn't wait to see how Jake fared on his trip back, nor did he let his attention linger on the motorboat racing downstream. He led the others into the brush and as far away from the river in the shortest amount of time that he could.

"Slow down, Nate!" Ivana said. "Nasty stickers are tearing my hair!" Ivana yanked herself away from another creosote bush.

"Do you two have any idea where we're at?" Jerry grumbled, swatting gnats from in front of his face.

"Ask her. She's a native. I've never been here in my life," Nathan answered, equally hot and irritated.

"Mexico," Ivana snickered. "And I haven't been here either, not in this wasteland."

They fought the bramble until the sun peeked up over the horizon. They had traveled beyond the low growing brush and now stumbled through a thicket of mesquite and ironwood. The stickers were no less plentiful.

"Do I look as bad as you do?" Nathan asked once first light revealed how dirty and ragged his friends were.

"Worse," Ivana snapped. She stopped, opened her purse, and rummaged through it.

"You came out of all that with your purse?" Jerry asked.

"A purse is part of a woman's body. It'd be like cutting off a limb if I left it behind. Everything I need is in here. My ID..." she pulled out her gum, "nutrients, my money, and my beauty!" She held up her compact."

"Good Lord!" Nathan mumbled. How can she worry about looks at a time like this? "How about water? Got any water in there? It's going to be a long hot walk in the desert when that sun comes all the way over the horizon."

"Water? Never touch the stuff."

Jerry laughed, but Ivana's face grew serious. "If my inner compass is right, there's a road nearby. I'm not sure exactly how far up river we came, but I think we crossed perpendicular to Papi's farm. I do know that if you stand in Papi's cornfield, there's a neighborhood on the States side you can see. I think that's where we were last night."

"We're trusting you on this one, Vana."

They trudged up a dusty hill out of the thicket when a cloud of dust skirted along the horizon. An old pickup truck emerged from the haze. "Look!"

"Hey, guys. That's José. What luck!" Ivana took off in a run waving her arms and calling out as the truck sped toward them. Nathan trailed behind, panting. The driver must have seen them well up the road, for he slowed, and then honked his horn. Ivana waved excitedly, her long black hair flying in the wind. No longer the tough teen behind a mask of makeup, Nathan couldn't help but notice how lovely she looked.

"What in the world...?" José asked as he jumped out of the truck and opened the door for Ivana.

"Am I ever glad to see you! This is Nate and Jerry. Take us home!"

Nathan wasted no time jumping into the back with Jerry. José spun the truck around and Nathan covered his face to protect himself from the dust as they sped off.

❖ ❖ ❖

"This is Papi's farm house." Filled with excitement, Ivana jumped from the cab, raced to the house, and pulled open the screen door. Nathan and Jerry had just climbed out of the bed of the truck, stepping quickly away from the two barking dogs that snapped at their heels.

"Hey Maddy, Ryon, stop!" José shouted at the pups, kicking up dirt to fend them off.

"And this is my brother, José." Used to her brother's spouts of anger, she introduced him with pride. "Be nice, José!"

Nathan returned José's nod.

"My sister says she smuggled you two across the border. This isn't a good place for you here. Not if you've got a warrant."

"José ...." Ivana interrupted.

"No. You risked your life going back to the States, and now you risk Papi and Aunt Flora's life returning with these people. It's good that you're safe, but I don't know, Vana. Hiding these two gringos can't be a good thing. You bring the Grays down on us from across the border then what? Then what happens to the farm?"

Ivana threw her hands on her hips. "What then? Were we supposed to let them shoot us? We didn't have any alternatives."

José gave Ivana a daggered look and walked inside. Ivana smiled at Nathan. Holding the screen door open she welcomed him in. "It's cool." Maybe her smile would make them feel welcome.

Nathan exchanged glances with Jerry.

"Come in and shut the door! Flies are getting inside." José yelled from the house.

"Look, Nate why don't you two go wash up and get a nap. Bathrooms down the hall. I'll talk to my brother. He'll be cool. He's just upset because Papi caught some kind of virus and is at the clinic in town. They'll be home this evening."

"Maybe there's something else we can do besides stay here."

"Nonsense. You'll stay here." Granted José was intimidating, but she wouldn't let her brother hurt Nathan and she sure wouldn't let him turn either of them away. She brushed dust off of Nathan's shirt and locked eyes with him. There was chemistry. Definitely. She smiled.

"I guess I don't have a lot of choices right now." Nathan wiped the sweat off his face.

"You'll be fine. José isn't as tough as he looks. C'mon, Jerry. You two are exhausted and I have some catching up to do with my family."

❖ ❖ ❖

It was the dogs barking that woke him.

When Nathan opened his eyes, the sun was low in the sky and the truck had just pulled in. He glanced around the room. Jerry lay on a cot snoring, his mouth open and eyes closed. Ivana was curled up on a couch in the other room, asleep. He heard the screen door slam and sat up on the bed.

The old man Ivana referred to as Papi entered the house. Thin and wiry, dark skin and smiling eyes, an older dark-haired woman followed. When José entered, the screen door slammed again.

"Vana, wake up! There's mail from Papa! It's addressed to you."

"Mail?"

Nathan rubbed the sleep from his eyes, and walked into the living room.

"Oh hi, Nate. This is my Auntie Flora," Ivana said as she retrieved the letter and bounced on the couch, hurriedly ripping the envelope open. Ambient light from the setting sun cast a sheen over the overstuffed davenport, and rustic rocking chair. Aunt Flora pulled the curtain open to see better. Ivana glanced at the parchment briefly and then read the back. "This isn't from Papa."

"It's from the States, from the military."

"It's from the prison down south. Look at the address." She showed him the envelope.

"It's addressed to you. What? That's not from Papa?"

"No." Ivana read the back again and looked at Nathan. "Oh, my God. It's from Abree!"

"Bree!" Nathan's heart leapt to his chest. He hadn't heard from his sister in months. He raced to Ivana's side and sat next to her, reading along as Ivana spoke the words.

Dear Ivana,

I hope this letter finds you and that you're well, as that was what Commander Garcia wanted. I didn't know how to address this letter so it'd get to you. I would have written my mom or Nate, but I heard that my brother is lost somewhere and that the Grays want to arrest him. I hope they don't. My mother is in a rest home somewhere. Things don't look very good for us. I am here in prison, but it's not so bad. Actually, your dad sent me here because he knew things would be better for me at this facility.

They are. I was working in this terrible lab where they made me poison people's food.

I am writing to you because you are the one person I might be able to locate. Your dad gave me this address and said you were probably on your way back to Mexico.

I hope you are sitting down because this news is going to be hard on you. The Grays came and arrested your father last night. They think he is smuggling seed out of the country.

*They don't know anything more about the smuggling ring
I don't think, or anything like that. But they have some
evidence against your dad and how he's been helping kids
like me, and they have security pictures of him stealing
corn. That's what the rumor is here, anyway. It doesn't
look good for him. I tried to find out where the Grays took
him, but we don't know yet. As soon as I find out I'll send
another letter. Makia and I are doing the best we can to
keep the seed coming through the tunnels. There are others
too, that are helping. We know it needs to get into the hands
of the farmers to save people from having to eat that awful
poison.*

*Don't worry. Your dad said you know about this and the
people who are taking my letter to you are part of the
Resistance.*

*I just wanted to let you know. If I could save him I would.
He is a very nice man and doesn't deserve to be in trouble.*

*If you ever see my brother again, would you tell him I love
him and I miss him?*

*Love
Abree Barber.*

"Bree is smuggling seed? What the hell is this about?" Nathan searched Ivana's eyes. He hadn't noticed José, Papi, and Aunt Flora standing around them. The whole room hung in silence. Ivana looked up.

"Papa's been arrested," she said.

José stormed out of the room. Ivana dropped clenched the letter and ran out after him. Aunt Flora fell on the couch wiping her brow with her scarf. Jerry scratched his head and mumbled.

Papi touched Nathan's arm and spoke softly. "Sometimes it is best to till the land and stay out of politics, but sometimes the world calls you to interfere."

"I can save Bree?" Nathan choked at the thought of his sister in prison.

Papi nodded. "You...." he pointed at Jerry, and outside where Ivana, and José had run off to. He tapped Nathan on the chest. "You four must do what you can for my son and your sister. Work together. Work hard and long, like my son has been. Work like the ants."

"How? How could we possible work against the Privatol? It's bigger than we are."

"Our people have a legend. We have always known that the Quetzalcoatl will be with us in these days. He brings us answers.There are stronger forces at work than what you see here."

Jerry stood at the door, arms folded, observing Ivana and José arguing outside. José jogged to the truck swinging his denim jacket over his shoulder. Ivana pulled on his arm and cried out in Spanish. He pushed her away and jumped in the cab, but Ivana stepped onto the running board. "Not alone! You can't do this by yourself. You'll be killed. You'll be captured."

"Get off the truck, Ivana." José started the engine.

"Nate!" Ivana yelled. Nathan ran after them as the truck crawled over the bumpy driveway. Ivana hung onto the mirror.

"Get down, Vana. I'm going to step on the gas. Get off!"

Nathan ran as fast as he could, breathing the trucks dust as it hobbled over the gravel. He hopped on the other running board and shouted through the open window.

"Good God, are you nuts? What are you doing? Listen to your sister, man. We can do this as a team. Jerry and I will help. Chill out!"

José beat on the steering wheel with his fist, and a low growl rumbled from his lips. "That's Papa they arrested. I won't let them take him. Maybe you don't care, Vana. How can these strangers care?"

"Damn right I care." Nathan could understand his anger, but José was dead wrong. "You think I want my baby sister in prison risking her life? I'm as mad as you are."

The truck slowed.

"Please, José," Ivana's pleaded through her tears. "No one wants Papa in jail."

"Jail. If it were just jail, it'd be different. They'll kill him, Vana. They'll give him a mock trial and then convict him and hang him as a traitor." He choked on his words and wiped his face.

"Then let's get a team together." Nathan unlatched the door and slid onto the seat. "Let's have a plan. If you just storm off across the border they'll arrest you. How will that help? Then we'll have to go find a way to save you."

José slammed on the brake. Ivana bounced onto the ground, but jumped on the running board again.

"What do you think I am? I'm no fool. I won't use the checkpoint. I'll go through the tunnels until I come to his cell."

"Tunnels?" Nathan wasn't sure he heard correctly.

"Great José, and then what will you do when you find him?" Ivana pressed.

Sweat dripped down José dark skin, his hair fell over his eyes and he brushed it away. "I don't know. Kill someone if I have to."

"What if we all went in the tunnels?" Ivana's voice lowered. "What if we got some people to come with us? Who do you have with you? Who else is a smuggler? Where are they? You know more than you've told me. You've always known more. That's why you didn't want me going back to the States, isn't it? You know about the tunnels. What else? What else do you know?"

"The seed comes here, Vana. That's what we've been harvesting. This is one of the farms that grow the seed. If the Grays find the farm they will destroy us all."

"Well, this field is pretty much in the open. I have to admit; your family is already vulnerable." Nathan stretched his neck above the pickup and surveyed the countryside. There was nothing for miles but the river, the windmill, and the rows of crops. One helicopter fly-over would discover the family all too easily.

"Not that vulnerable. We have friends."

Nathan laughed. "What kind of friends?"

"I can't talk about it." A moment passed as Nathan and Ivana both looked to José for a change of heart. Finally, José dropped his guard. "We'll do it your way then. We'll go back to the house and think it out, but time is slipping, you know? We can't waste it by talking. We have to act."

"I love you, José." Ivana leaned through the window and grabbed his head, kissing his hair.

He blushed and pushed her away. "Stop it, Vana. You'll get your way, already!"

❖ ❖ ❖

Whether Papi had planned to serve them all cocoa before they left in a fury, Nathan wasn't sure. It seemed the old man knew José would return to the house. Still, when the group of young people walked inside, Papi showed them his grin. He set the cups on the table and nodded toward the chairs, beginning his lecture with a smile. "Only the wild hare rushes off at the slightest sign of danger," Papi began. "Doing so alerts the hunter and soon the hare is nothing but stew on the table."

Ivana looked at José.

"Not so with the wise man. There is always a solution to any problem. We have to say to ourselves, what is the best way to tackle this one?" He cleared his throat. "How would nature remedy this? For instance, if there were a dam, and the river wanted to run free, what would nature do? Think about that? You see how it's the same? You have a dam of sorts, our family held prisoner like the great waters of the Rio Grande."

"Nature'd probably toss out a big storm, lots of lightning, flood the river till it couldn't hold the river back any longer. Then the dam would burst. That's what I think, anyway." Jerry pushed his chair in, eager for the cocoa. "If you want my opinion."

"The Grays dammed the river," José said.

"Where?" There was alarm in Ivana's voice.

"West of here. Not to stop it, but to change its course. The tunnels that the Resistance uses go under the old river bed."

"Why? Why did they dam the river?"

"To keep the American farmers from growing. To devastate the land. Control. They stop at nothing."

"So, the Resistance has taken advantage of this misfortune?" Jerry asked distracted by the tortillas that Papi set on the table.

"The Resistance digs deep. Their tunnel connects to the basements of three facilities, maybe four. We have people in all of them."

"Children? Like Abree?"

"*Si.* Little ones. And Grays, like Papa. Not everyone believes in the Privatol. The children volunteer. They've been the targets of the Grays propaganda and many feel strongly in their heart that they are doing the right thing. Never underestimate the power of a child. They are fast, persistent, and intuitive."

Nathan nodded in agreement; the image of his freckled face sister came to mind. He had to free her. He had to get her away from there. "I'm with you, José. We need to get this done." They were silent as they passed the condiments: homemade salsa, beans, chopped vegetables. The food tasted good and settled Nathan's stomach, though his chewing was rushed. He wanted to hurry. "José, do you know where this prison is, the one Bree is in? Where her letter came from? Do you know which tunnel goes there?"

"It's not far from the border, maybe five miles at the most. I know where it is. It's the closest one. I know those tunnels like the back of my hand."

Hope restored, Nathan laughed. "You mean you could take us to where Bree is? Just like that?"

"I can take you to the facility's tunnels. Maybe you'll see your sister, I don't know. Maybe not. We don't see all the runners when we go. Just some of them, but they'd know where she is. It's a small prison. Everyone knows everyone there."

"So, we could free her then?" Nathan bit his lip, the energy too difficult to contain.

José looked at him. "What do you want? To take her away from what she's doing? To bring her to Mexico to stay with us?" José snickered and pushed his plate away.

Of course, he did. Why did José protest? Couldn't he understand?

Nathan was speechless.

"José!" Ivana reached across the table and grabbed José's arm. "He wants to see his little sister. He wants to know she's okay. What does it matter after that? Let him be."

"Pfft!" José stood. "No one is okay in this world anymore. No one."

Papi rested his hand on José's shoulder. "What troubles you, troubles all of us. Look at our friends here, grandson. Don't you see the same worry on their faces? Eh?" Papi's smile broadened as he encouraged him, catching José's eyes. "Today we're family. Maybe not blood. What does it matter? God put us together to do a job."

The stiff air softened as José relaxed and glanced at Nathan. With Papi patting him on the back, Ivana's brother held out his hand. Nathan met his handshake.

"We'll work together." Nathan could tell José was embarrassed and humbled; he refused to make eye contact. "We're on the same side," was all Nathan uttered.

"Good. Now that's settled, let's devise a plan!" Jerry said cheerfully.

Search for Abree

José killed the engine. He had been driving with no headlamps for almost a mile, guided only by starlight. The sound of the river was near enough that Nathan could still hear it, although they had traveled half a mile into the dry riverbed, away from the Rio's altered course. No one spoke. Chatter of crickets sang a chorus that seemed to echo off the stars. The cab door creaked when José stepped out and pulled a rifle from behind the seat. Nathan and Jerry both peeked from under the tarp.

"Let's go," José whispered.

Ivana slipped out of the cab and met Nathan with a smile. "This is it, Nate. We might see Abree tonight!"

"Shh," José warned.

Nathan returned Ivana's grin. The hope of seeing his little sister after all these months of separation brought purpose to this venture. He knew he was risking his life, yet to do so in hopes that Abree would be freed, made the risk worthwhile.

Jerry adjusted the backpack on his shoulders. "Chemist accounted for."

José led the way through the sandy wash. The banks to the old riverbed grew steep. Roots and branches still held the muddy walls in place and reeds poked at the sky, now brown and wilting. Changing the course of the Rio Grande was a crime. So much of the southwest depended on this river-so much good farmland had been ruined.

"Think of the wildlife that died because of this dam," Ivana whispered. "It's despicable."

"Here!" José stopped near a terrain that had once been backwaters, an island-like jetty with a bank as tall as they were. "File in one at a time. It's treacherous at first, but once you hit hardpan it will be easier to walk."

Jerry went first. Headlamp lit, he crouched low through. José leaned over the hole and called to him. "It drops off. Be careful. There are steps, but they aren't very wide."

"I see." Jerry answered with a muffled voice.

Nathan was next. The hole was narrow, and the sand loose, but the hard wood frame was newly constructed and seemed safe. He hung onto each rung as he lowered himself, using the light on Jerry's headlamp as a guide. Twenty-two steps brought him to the bottom, a hard-cold ground that smelled like wet earth.

Ivana came after Nathan, and then another lamp. The light from José's headlamp flashed in his eyes so bright that Nathan had to turn aside and blink away the spots.

"What's that sound?" Jerry asked, a tremble in his voice. Nathan heard it too. A low rumble much like a train but constant, a tremor drawing neither nearer nor farther.

"That's the river." José was nonchalant, as though he'd heard the same rumble often. He moved past them and took the lead.

"This is a pretty elaborate tunnel for having been built so recently." Ivana inspected the narrow passage as José's lamp lit the dirt walls surrounding them.

"Not so recent," José mumbled.

"Well, it's only been a few years since the Privatol invaded our countries."

"This part under the river bed is new, but the rest of the tunneling has been in place for years. The entrance was at a different location before."

"You know all that? Cool. What do people use it for?" Somehow Ivana had found a stick of gum to chew on. José glanced at her, but didn't answer.

"Well?" She pressed him.

"Anything they want." Her brother snickered and walked on.

"Crossing the border illegally?" Jerry asked.

"Could be." José moved quicker, creating a distance from his three followers.

"Hey!" Ivana jogged to keep up. "You're awfully secretive. What gives with that? Why don't you just let us in on what's going on? Nate and Jerry are our friends, José. They're here to help. And frankly, I'm tired of your secrets. Have some respect. I'm your sister!"

José stopped and gave her a hard stare, which Ivana took calmly, popping her gum at him, her arms folded across her chest. Sensing trouble, Nathan stood by Ivana's side, distracting José for only a moment.

"You really want to know what's going on with this place? With me? With the farm?"

"It would help, yeah. Hell, if we're going to be risking our lives it'd be nice to know."

José switched his rifle to his other hand. "Okay. I'll tell you. Rondo. That's what's happening."

"Rondo?" Ivana gasped. "Get out of here. What does Rondo have to do with anything?"

"Who's Rondo?" Jerry asked.

"The town bully," Ivana sneered. "This is his tunnel?"

"He's more than a bully, Ivana. He's in with the Cartel now. He's a drug lord."

"So...we're in a drug tunnel, so to speak?" Jerry looked around nervously.

"Drugs and illegals, but if you stay with me you won't get shot."

"And this is the tunnel Bree uses? My little sister in a tunnel with drug traffickers?"

José resumed his trek into the dark foreboding alley way under the earth, his back to them. "The kids don't come this far. We have runners from this side that meet them closer in."

"I can't believe this. Rondo smuggling seed?"

"Sometimes. Not always. Sometimes Rondo's gang comes here if there's a problem"

"Unbelievable." Nathan muttered under his breath, appalled at the idea that Abree was involved with not only the Grays, but drug lords.

José stopped short and faced Nathan, fury in his eyes. "What is unbelievable?"

"That Bree is mixed up with lowlifes."

"Is that right? Well I don't know what you're thinking, because those Grays are doing a lot more harm to the kids in your country than any drug lord around here."

"José!" Ivana grabbed his arm. "C'mon. Not now. You know they're all crude. You've seen what Rondo's done."

"Yeah, Vana. I have. Well, it's Rondo that keeps our farm going. Without his gang, the Grays would have invaded the border by now. Without his help, you'd be eating the Privatol's poison, too. All of us would."

"José!"

"Okay. I concede." Nathan interrupted Ivana, fearing that her anger would make things worse. "You're right. Chill out! Maybe your friends are the better of the two evils. I was wrong in judging them."

"I'll say," Jerry interrupted. "Let's just get on with this mission before we all kill each other. There's something important for us to do, and I'm getting the willies being underground like this. Especially hearing that river so close by. What if…."

"Don't even think it, Jerry!" Ivana gave him a dirty look. "We're perfectly safe. Aren't we, José?"

"Perfectly."

It came out more a sneer: a snide utterance that meant the opposite of what Ivana and Jerry were hoping. Nathan considered it a warning. Something was darkly dangerous about this venture and José was not making the atmosphere any lighter.

Nathan's steps were more reserved. It didn't matter that José was so far ahead he lost sight of him at times. Ivana walked behind her brother for a while and then dropped behind with Nathan. Jerry closed the gap. It was Jerry's lamp that Nathan and Ivana could see by.

"Things are going to work out, Nate. We'll get your sister." Ivana spoke softly, but her attempt at comforting had little effect.

"You can promise that?"

"You know the answer to that, but what good is it to be negative?"

"I don't know, Vana. The whole idea of rescuing Bree is so abstract. Your brother doesn't really know where she is. And he's so dead set in finding your dad that I wonder if Bree is even a priority."

"We talked about it in the truck on our way here. José said Bree might know where Papa is. The letter said she was going to try and find out. Maybe she had time. My brother wants to find Bree as much as you do."

"For questioning."

"Isn't that enough?" She slowed, taking Nathan's hand. Jerry and his light soon left them in the dark.

"I just don't see it. I don't see us getting out of this mess. The Grays are everywhere, and they'd be happy to get their hands on me. And you, too. I wonder if they found the van."

"No. They didn't find the van."

"How do you know?"

Ivana smiled smugly. "Because Melinda promised me Jake was going to drive it to the nearest bank, put it in neutral and run it off a cliff into the river. No one will find it except maybe some fisherman someday."

Nathan returned her smile but only for a moment.

"Look Nate, I never told you about Quetzalcoatl."

"Your grandpa did."

"He did?"

"Yes, he did. He took me aside while you were begging your brother to stop the truck."

"I wasn't begging."

"Whatever. Your Papi explained to me that there are stronger forces

163

working in the universe than just us. He told me there are things we needed to do, and that we needed to be a team. So here we are doing them. Team? Not so much."

"Did he tell you to find the ant people?"

"No. He said to follow them. Evidently they've already been found."

"Yeah? Where?"

Nathan chuckled. "Where do you think? Underground." He squeezed her hand, earning a turn of her head. "It's the team part I'm worried about. I don't get where your brother is coming from."

She pulled away, her dark eyes pinning him. "He's my brother. What does it matter?"

"Holy Shit!" Jerry appeared suddenly leaping toward them. Nathan and Ivana dodged for cover. Gunfire echoed through the tunnel, staggered pops and bullets ricocheting near their heads. José pulled back behind a post, aiming his rifle, but he didn't shoot.

The men in the shadows shouted, but Nathan couldn't understand them. They weren't speaking Spanish, but rather the language of the Privatol's Army. Nathan pulled Ivana closer to him and covered her with his body. The guys that wanted to hang him were shooting at him.

José inched along the wall that Nathan, Ivana, and Jerry clung too. He waved to them to retreat. Their lamps off, the tunnel was black as night. Another shot hit the wall across from them. José motioned for them to move quicker.

"I have an idea," Jerry whispered. No one else dare to speak. "You guys run. Let the chemist work."

It wasn't supposed to happen like this, but Jerry had insisted they have an alternate plan. Nathan's eye's locked onto Jerry's briefly. No telling how many Grays were out there, and how far they would follow. Nathan pushed Ivana and pulled at José.

"Run!" he whispered.

Shots fired out when they skipped into the center of the tunnel. Nathan looked back at Jerry only once. The jars were clear of the pack taped together and rolling toward the center of the tunnel. Jerry caught up to him and the two raced past Ivana. José stopped and turned aiming his rifle at the jars. He fired. Shards of glass bounced and ricocheted followed by a steamy yellow mist that spiraled in the air and filled the tunnel.

"Cover your nose and get the hell out of here," Nathan ordered.

There were no more gunshots. No one would survive those fumes. As much as it hurt Nathan's lungs, he ran. His pace synchronized with the others, galloping toward the tunnel entrance, the four reached the ray of moonlight shining on the stairwell.

Rondo

Nathan staggered out of the tunnel into the fresh night air, aching from the fumes he had breathed and his head dizzy from the gas. The fresh air filled his lungs that now burned with hyperventilation. He wheezed, caught his equilibrium, and then fell in front of the entrance. "Ivana!"

"I'm coming."

Nathan reached out to help Ivana up the last stair, giving her a healthy pull to the outside.

"What the…?" Ivana leaned over as she coughed. "What the hell was in those jars?"

"Drano in one, bleach in the other." Jerry, having been the first one out, paced anxiously around the sage brush while waiting for José.

"My God it was awful," Ivana said.

"I bet the Grays think so too." Nathan spat the unsavory taste out of his mouth. "You okay?"

Ivana nodded. "I'll survive now that I'm out of there."

José appeared, slinging his rifle over his shoulder and breaking into a run. "Get to the truck. Hurry."

Jerry took the lead. Nathan ran as well as he could, though breathing was still difficult. Ivana fared worse, lagging and coughing. With a steady arm, Nathan supported her and the two returned to the truck arm in arm.

José had already started the engine of the old pickup. Nathan opened the door for Ivana and helped her in. If he hadn't jumped in the back as fast as he did, he would have been left behind. As it were, he nearly fell off the tailgate when José stepped on the gas.

Dust rose in the sky as the pickup burned rubber, turned sharply and bounded its way cross-country until it hit the road. Hard.

"We aren't going back to the farm?" Jerry asked. Neither Jerry nor Nathan pulled the tarp over their heads, but rather watched the night fly by.

"It doesn't appear that way. José isn't stupid. It'd be crazy to lead the Grays back to their farm."

"You think they're following us?"

Nathan shrugged, watching the riverbed as they distanced themselves from it. There was no sign of anyone pursuing them. "Who knows?"

"So, where do you think we're going?"

With the truck rattling and shaking, Nathan held onto the side of the bed as he stretched his neck beyond the cab. When the pickup cleared an incline, lights of a town glowing on the horizon appeared.

"Looks like we might be headed for Del Rio."

Nathan tolerated the bumpy ride and the cool air blowing on his face. A ride in the back of the pickup was a welcome relief from the stuffy tunnel, bullets flying, and poisonous gas filling his lungs. In fact, it was enjoyable. Nathan smiled. His friend didn't seem to understand at first, but then Jerry broke into a laugh.

"That was a pretty close call, Nate. I don't know how many adventures like that I can live through."

"I'll be happy once Bree is out of danger." Nathan's smile disappeared. Poor Bree was still in that prison, still with those soldiers and their twisted ways.

Jerry gave him a nod, accentuated by the rocking truck. "Me too."

Once they passed the last of the mesquite forest, the silhouette of date palms against the sleepy sky drew near. The road smoothed, and scattered houses appeared under dimly lit, old-fashioned streetlights. Rotten smells of sewer and garbage greeted them: the stench of a dying town. The truck slowed as it meandered through the city streets. Abandoned businesses, their windows and doors barred with iron, lined the road. José pulled the truck into a dusty parking lot in front of a faded turquoise building, the stucco crumbling at the corners and a vintage beer sign written in Spanish flickered above the door.

"Wait here." José slammed the truck door and walked inside.

"Oh boy," Jerry whispered under his breath. "What is this? The Sundance Kid's hide out?"

Nathan snickered. "The ghost of the Sundance kid maybe."

The haunting atmosphere mixed with the chill of dawn caused a shiver to run up Nathan's back. He looked through the rear window at Ivana. Still chewing gum, she was applying lipstick, using the rearview mirror and the dim light of the bar sign to see by. She smiled at him looking at her. He couldn't help but smile back. His fondness for Ivana grew by the day.

A dust devil vacuumed the street sending scraps of paper into the air. That and the bark of a dog broke the silence. Several other neon signs suggested life still existed in the little town, although Nathan saw none.

"This place is creepy." Jerry shuddered and pulled the tarp up to his shoulders.

"No lie."

The door to the turquoise cantina opened. José appeared and whistled, signaling them to join him. Ivana was the first one out of the truck. Nathan and Jerry followed although not nearly as eagerly.

Nathan had never been in Mexico before. His mother had told him stories about her honeymoon that she and his dad had taken back in the days when their love was young. Sunny beaches, delicious food, and a golden ocean cruise were memories she had promised Nathan she'd experience again. "Maybe I could take you and Bree someday," she once told him wistfully.

This was not that same Mexico.

Stepping inside was like walking into an old movie, but lacking the glamour of Hollywood. The place smelled of spilled alcohol and tobacco ashes. Round tables marked up with notches, a smoldering fireplace, and hurricane lamps breathing smoke furnished the room. Crouching under the low ceiling Nathan followed José to a corner where a thin, dark-skin man waited, his boot heels on a table, his chair pushed back on two legs, and his arms folded across his chest. He wore blue jeans and a dark flannel shirt. A pitted face, there was nothing warm or inviting about his countenance. His eyes followed Ivana before they found Nathan and Jerry.

José sat across from the man. They conversed in Spanish for a long while and Ivana broke in several times before her brother waved her to be silent. She looked at Nathan, but he could give no input, and to ask for a translation, seemed inappropriate.

"You!" The man nodded at Nathan who sat erect. "You're the outlaw then. The reason for my comrade and his family's trouble?"

"It's not like that, Rondo." Ivana shifted in her chair, her anger stirring. "We're all in trouble on our own. Don't blame him. The Gray soldiers are to blame. You know that."

Rondo pulled his legs off the table and dropped his chair back onto the floor. After taking a swig from his beer, he wiped his mouth with his arm. "What do you want, José? I already keep the Grays off your land, away from your farm. What are you coming to me for?"

"Help us free Papa. They arrested him."

"No. No border crossing. You know that."

"You don't have to cross. We'll cross."

Rondo held out his arms. "Then what?"

"We need guns."

Nathan's eyes grew wide. This was not in the script. A gunfight was the last thing he wanted, especially after this last go around. He never even shot a gun, much less killed anyone.

"Oh man," Jerry mumbled and rolled his eyes.

Rondo took another swig of beer. "I need my guns. Besides, any day now we'll all be cut off."

"What do you mean?" Nathan asked. Rondo turned sharply and stared at him, his unshaven scowl slowly creasing into a grin. "They are going to loose the dam, man. That's what I mean."

Shock took Nathan's breath.

"What the hell are you saying?" José asked.

"The Grays. They know about your father. They know about the smuggling. They are letting the waters run. Soon. Maybe the day after tomorrow the flood will come. There will be no tunnel. It will all be at the river bottom. For people like you, there will be no way in or out of your country."

"How do you know that?" Ivana's eyes filled with anger. "You're making that up!"

He laughed. "Last week my men were there to meet a runner, but instead the Grays showed up in the tunnel. There was a shootout." He laughed. "My men got one of them, but curious, they had to find out more. Why are the Gray soldiers in the smuggling tunnel, you know? So, they followed them. They spied." Rondo grinned as his eyes darted to each of them. Maybe Rondo liked being the deliverer of bad news. He spoke to Ivana. "My men listen carefully when they are on a mission, *mi Corazon*. Maybe you should, too." He looked at Nathan. "Your sister in that prison?" He shook his head slowly, speaking words that stung Nathan to the heart. "She will not escape. It's too late." He licked his lips and turned to José. "Your Papa will die, too."

"Hogwash!" José pushed his chair from the table when he stood.

Rondo chuckled, rubbing his beer bottle against his lips.

"Help us, Rondo." Ivana slapped her hands on the table, startling the drug lord so suddenly his beer splashed on his shirt. "Our farm is just as important to you and your family as it is to us. You know that. The whole town needs our crops. Stop playing games."

Rondo set his bottle down after studying each of them again; he pointed his finger at José. "You. You and I will talk. Alone."

Twenty-Four Hours

The transporter drove away. A cloud of dust trailed behind as sunlight bounced off the chrome of the vehicle's body. The Gray's truck vanished into a flatland blanketed with thorn bushes and mesquite, leaving behind a handful of children, abandoned in the desolate desert.

Abree felt the heat of anger more than she felt the heat of the sun. Most of her friends were crying. Still in their prison-greens the three other girls huddled in the brush seeking shade. The boys stood dazed, like Abree and Makia, watching the truck drive away.

The ride hadn't been long. The riverbed was only a few miles from the prison. Still, it had been hot and miserable in the truck, and the group had to wait in a tiny cell before they were even escorted outside. And then they had to wait in the dust under the hot sun for the truck to show up. The Grays were wicked, especially Jenkins who had sneered at Abree the whole trip.

"You know what they're going to do to you, don't you?" she had asked. "You have less than twenty-four hours after they drop you off." She laughed. Abree turned away from the officer and avoided her eyes the rest of the trip.

With Commander Garcia arrested and the smuggling ring revealed, the prison had been evacuated. Anyone suspected of being a runner was put in the transporter and driven out to the desert, left to the elements in the dried-up riverbed of the Rio Grande.

Abree joined the four girls that sat despondent in the sand. She knelt next to Patricia, a redhead who used to live in south Sunrise. She had gone to a different school than Abree, but their classes met last year during a choir competition and sing-along. Patty and Abree had lunch together and became friends. Those were the fun days.

"Don't cry, Patty." Abree gave her a hug. Patricia clung to Abree and wept on her shoulder—her body shivered sporadically.

"We're going to die," Patty said as she wiped her face on Abree's sleeve. "We're going to die a long and grueling death. I just know it."

"No, we're not." Makia stood over them with the other three boys. "We're not going to die, but we need to go." Makia looked around anxiously, drawing Abree's attention.

"Go where?"

"Find shelter. Find water."

"The river's a good mile from here at the least. We'll never make it. Look at everyone. We're already sunburned."

"We'll find a place to dig. With the river nearby, water can't be far down."

"Makia, get real. How are we going to dig for water?"

"Abree, you aren't thinking. Men have always found water by either scouting for a stream or digging. We need to find a shady place and dig for water. The roots of the trees will show us where."

"Seriously?" Patty had stopped crying and wiped her eyes.

"Yes. I'm serious." He turned to Abree. "What has been our guide? Tell me. Are you going to give up and die? Or will you let the ant people save us?"

"The ant people? If I hear you talk about ant people one more time I'm going to scream." Abree was tired of Makia's legends and fairytales. There were no ant people. There were ants, but they weren't people. They were bugs and certainly not intelligent enough to guide anyone.

"If you scream, the coyotes will find us."

Sweat dripped down Makia's face, the drops caking in balls of dust.

His eyes were red, his hair matted, the shine gone. She must look as bad as he did.

"Fine. I won't scream. So where is there a shady spot? These bramble trees don't offer much shade."

"There are cottonwoods closer to the river." Makia pointed southeast. Though Abree couldn't see the tall shimmering leaves of the refreshing cottonwoods now, she had seen them from her window in prison.

"Are you sure that's the direction of the river?"

"Yes. Look at this wash. It heads toward the sun, doesn't it? This is the old riverbed. It must lead to the Rio Grande.

Patricia stood and joined the group that had gathered around Makia.

"We'll walk up that way for a little while and take cover when we're tired." Makia pointed southeast. "Come on!"

"Lead the way, Makia." Johnny Kruell was taller than everyone in the group, but he was also smart. Makia talked highly of Johnny many times when bragging about the runners, saying Johnny was the strongest and quickest of everyone, and he could also be the sneakiest. Now Johnny showed Makia respect by asking him to lead. It had to make Makia proud. Abree smiled. She was proud of Makia, too.

"Okay, then let's go." Abree gave Patty a hand up as the other girls stood. Anything would be better than sitting around this pit by the road brooding over their misfortune. "We are, after all, the Resistance, aren't we?" Abree grinned. "Well let's resist the Gray's plan to do away with us. Let's survive!"

Her words lifted everyone's spirits. They marched up the riverbed, arm in arm, dusting each other's clothes with a friendly pat on the back.

❖ ❖ ❖

No clouds offered relief from the sun, not even for a moment as sometimes they do. The only activity around them were the heat waves that shimmered in the sand. The riverbed was difficult to walk in, stony in parts, huge boulders in others. No shade and a blaring sun could be dangerous and Abree kept an eye on her friends. With the humidity of the river air, sunstroke was a grave probability. Fortunately for Abree, Nathan had taught her about sunstroke when he took her on hikes in the park. She knew the signs. Dizziness, vomiting. "How does everyone feel?" Abree asked.

"I miss my home," Patty answered immediately. "If I were home, I'd be in an air-conditioned house playing with my dog, Pepper. Poor Pepper."

Abree hadn't meant the question in that context, but if someone had felt ill, she was sure they would have said so. "I miss home, too." Abree dare not ask what happened to Patty's dog. The Grays did horrible things when they invaded their town. "Mostly I miss my mom and Nathan."

"I miss playing baseball." Johnny swung at the air and watched his imaginary home run by shading the sun from his eyes. "And visiting my grandma. She always had chocolate chip cookies."

"Yeah, cookies," Peter, a short boy with lots of teeth pouted. "I could do with a cookie. Did those guys that dropped us off leave anything at all to eat?"

"Forget it, Pete. If they had, it would have been gray mash and we wouldn't want it anyway," Johnny answered as he waited for Pete to catch up. "We'll find something to eat. Jojoba berries if nothing else."

"Yuk!" Patty stuck out her tongue. "Jojoba berries taste awful."

"But they are good for you and will keep you alive." Leave it to Makia to contribute wisdom. Abree smiled. He was more practical than anyone she ever met, and knew all about surviving. She was glad he was here.

"I can't wait to find some." Abree looked ahead wondering if she'd know what a Jojoba bean plant looked like as they followed the meandering riverbed. Every plant was beginning to look the same. Her head was hot from the sun, her lips parched. Patty had fallen behind, and her steps were getting shorter and shorter. When Abree fell back to walk with her, she noticed the girl's eyes were rolling back into her head.

"Are you all right?"

"Yeah." Patty said, and then her legs crumbled under her. Abree screamed and Makia came running.

"Get her out of the sun!"

Makia and the boys pulled Patty to the bank, Abree at the girl's side, unbuttoned her sleeves and rolled them up. Makia dug at the bank and grabbed a handful of damp earth.

"Don't look!" She scolded the boys. She unbuttoned Patty's jumpsuit and loosened the Harley bandana she had hidden in her sleeve, tied around her arm, a relic she refused to let the Gray's confiscate. She filled it with the mud that Makia had brought, making a cool poultice to put on Patty's head. She rested it there, quietly thanking Nathan for giving her his bandana. "We have to wait here. We're all so thirsty."

Every one of the children sat down next to Patty, waving their hands to make a breeze. The sun was setting and with it the temperature of the day cooled. "Maybe we should rest."

"I vote we sleep here for the night. We're all tired. None of us have had any sleep since they arrested us. Look at everyone. We'll make much better time in the morning." It was Johnny being diplomatic, persuading his case, as if he had to convince someone.

"We can rest," Makia agreed, "but tonight I'm going to dig for water. You all can help me if you want. At least there is cool mud nearby. It means the water table is high. Once we sleep we'll be fine. Tomorrow we'll be at the river where we can bathe and fish."

"Fish?" Peter looked to him for more encouragment. "I know how to catch catfish with my hands. My uncle showed me."

"Boy! I would like to learn how to do that," Johnny said.

"I'll teach you."

Talk of getting to the river got everyone excited again. Even Patty opened her eyes and color came back to her. Abree listened to the others, glad for them, but then a sick feeling moved in her stomach. Maybe she was getting sunstroke too, or maybe being out in the desert with no food and water was wearing her down emotionally. Or maybe it was the worry she had bottled up over what Jenkins had said just before Abree stopped listening to her. "You have less than twenty-four hours after they drop you off…."

"Twenty-four hours?" she mumbled. Maybe Makia would have the answer to that riddle.

Makia looked at her. "What?"

She stood, and pulled him away from the others so that they could talk privately. "Jenkins said we have less than twenty-four hours after they drop us off."

"And then what?"

"I don't know. That's all she said, and then she laughed her evil laugh and that was the end of it."

"No one starves to death in twenty-four hours," Makia assured her.

"I know."

"And remember in Biology we learned man can live for up to ten days without water? Maybe in this heat it could be less, but not twenty-four hours. And even the sun will be down soon, and it won't be so hot. I'm sure I'll find water before that. "

"You're right. What's happening in twenty-four hours, Makia? I don't think she meant starving or dying from thirst. I think she meant something else. What?"

Water in the Desert

❝Wake up!" Ivana shook Nathan. "Come on. What's wrong with you? We don't have time to be lazy." She had more on her mind than the sun coming up. She'd seen the vision again; Quetzalcoatl came to her last night and demanded she find the ant people. Again! What a crazy nightmare, but it wouldn't stop and she woke up frantic. José was nowhere to be found, but his truck was still outside in the parking lot at the cantina, and Nathan was asleep in the back. Where Jerry was, she didn't know.

"Why didn't we leave last night?" Nathan grumbled, brushing his hair with his hands.

"Everyone fell asleep. I had a nightmare, and time is running out. If we don't get past the tunnel under the riverbed today, there won't be a tunnel and we'll never get to rescue your sister."

'Where is José?"

"I don't know. Let's just go."

"What, and take his truck?"

"You can hotwire it. Let José stay with his cartel friends. I'm mad at him. Who knows what he's doing."

"Right, Vana. Hotwire your brother's truck while he's hanging out with the drug lords, who just happen to carry around machine guns, are trigger-happy, and hate white boys who hang with their sisters."

"Come on, Nate. Let's just go. Do you want to save Abree or not?"

"Yes, I want to save Abree." Nathan jumped to the ground as Ivana opened the passenger door.

"Then hot wire the truck and let's go!" She jumped inside as Nathan open the driver's door.

"And when your brother starts shooting at me?"

"Duck. Maybe they'll hit a Gray instead."

"Right. Duck and jump both at the same time. Once from the Grays, and once from your brother." Nathan fiddled with the steering column, and discovered a set of wires near the dash. "Hey! That's easy."

"What?"

"This truck has already been hotwired." Nathan touched the wires together and the engine revved. "You think you can find that tunnel entrance?"

"Follow the tracks we made last night." Ivana took the fresh pack of gum she'd picked up at the cantina out of her purse and unwrapped a stick, offering it to Nathan. He took it and popped it in his mouth. She smiled.

"This isn't so bad," Nathan steered the pickup out of town at an easy pace. "Nice ride, pretty girl, lots of country side, on a mission to save my baby sister. I could get into this!"

"Well, that's good to know because you're into it, all right. We both are. This is a do or die kind of thing, you know?"

"Yep. I know. So, what do you think? Do you think we'll do, or will we die?"

Ivana shrugged as she watched the date palms and fading telephone poles pass by. A backward country, Del Rio had little that the modern world in America offered, and yet it was home. She felt a lot of love right now. Love for her homeland, for her family. Even for Nathan. She liked being by him. And then that feeling of love disintegrated into remorse. They were in trouble, all of them. The whole world was in trouble. She could die today and she didn't want to die. She'd miss all of this: the desert, Papi's farm, Papi and José and Auntie Flora- that is if you miss anything when you die. She wiped a tear that was crawling down her cheeks. "Man!"

"What?"

"Nothing, Just nothing. Just drive and let's find little Abree before they flood the basin, blasted Grays."

Nathan stepped on the gas.

They drove out of town until it seemed they might be getting close, from what Ivana could remember. When the palm trees disappeared, and forests of mesquite stretched across the countryside, Nathan let up on the gas. "How are we going to find it, Vana? How'd your brother know where it was?"

"He's been there a million times I suppose." Ivana stuck her head out the window; the warm air grabbed her hair and flapped it against her face. "Wait. Stop."

Nathan pulled over and Ivana jumped out of the truck and walked to the driver's side. "Go slow." She stepped onto the running board. "There's got to be tracks where he came out last night. Got to be." Her heart beat with anxiousness.

The truck crept along the quiet road. Not a lot of traffic out here. The road didn't go anywhere for all she knew. Just desert. Maybe at a river bend somewhere. Ivana didn't know. She never went any farther than Papi's farm. She held on to the large side-view mirror and set her eyes on the opposite shoulder of the road. "Any traces of tire marks, ruts, skids. Stop!"

"What do you see?"

"There. Tracks. Turn around."

Nathan did a three-point turn and pulled up to the shoulder.

"This is it, man. I'm sure of it."

"I hope you're right because if you aren't and we get stuck…."

"We won't get stuck."

"You are always so sure of yourself." Nathan put the truck in low and took it over the shallow ditch, over the tumbleweeds and into the dunes. When he got to solid ground he stopped. "Get inside."

Ivana jumped off the running board and slid inside next to him. He stepped on the gas. "The ground is soft in spots. If I don't get going, we'll get stuck. So, hang on!"

The wheels skidded and smoke puffed from the tail pipe. Ivana's head hit the roof and she bounced on the seat as the pickup charged through the bumpy terrain. When it came to sand in the riverbed, the wheels bore down and stopped.

"We're stuck."

"I don't think we're far from the entrance. Let's walk."

"When did Rondo say they were going to release the dam waters?"

"His buddy was pretty sure it would be this afternoon, maybe around 3."

"You talked to his buddy?"

"Yep. After you left the cantina, José took us upstairs. All his buddies were up there."

"What happened to Jerry?"

"I don't know. I thought he was with you. Let's go, Nate."

"What time is it?"

Ivana pulled her cell from her purse. "7 a.m."

Nathan put the truck in reverse. The tires spun before they grabbed hold of hard earth. He quickly maneuvered the vehicle onto to solid ground. Ivana slammed the door and jogged next to Nathan as they followed the foot tracks through the wash.

She hadn't been too uncomfortable this morning while in the truck, but now, walking in the steamy riverbed, gnats found her face, buzzing into her eyes and nose unmercifully. She slapped at them, swearing under her breath. Aside from the pests, the silence was unusually heavy, as if the Earth was waiting for something to happen. Ivana knew what it was. "What the hell is this? The calm before the storm or something?" she asked.

Nathan broke into a run when they came to the embankment. It wasn't hard to see the hole in the ground. The dark tunnel stood out like an inkblot on a white piece of paper. Ivana felt the sun's heat on the back of her head as she watched Nathan crawl inside.

"Does it still stink in there?"

"A little. You might want to cover your face with something."

Ivana put her hand over her nose and followed him into the dark, dreading every step. The smell of the chlorine gas still lingered, but enough fresh air had seeped into the tunnel to counteract the dangerous fumes. Once at the bottom of the stairs, Ivana reached out to a wall, and following the passageway by touch, she inched forward. Nathan was not far ahead.

"You want to hold my hand?" His voice was gentle, and she knew he meant the gesture in kindness, yet it seemed odd to Ivana to have him ask.

"I'm not a kid."

"No. You aren't."

He didn't pursue the offer and she was glad. She'd much rather be free to turn and run if they happened on a bullet speeding at them.

Nathan stopped suddenly.

"Don't do that! You almost made me trip." She stumbled and gained her balance by grabbing his shirt.

"Can you see anything?"

Ivana opened her eyes as wide as she could. Her night vision was working, but there wasn't much to see. And then she realized that Nathan was referring to a wall of dirt in front of them. Lumber and the posts that had held the tunnel up were destroyed, heaped into a pile of debris lying at their feet.

"They blocked us off."

"No way!"

"Let's go back."

There wasn't much else to do. Ivana led, quicker than they had entered. Though she wished there was a way to find Abree, she was glad she didn't encounter the Grays in the tunnel.

"What's plan B this time?" Ivana asked as they crawled into the sunlight. Not a lot of time had passed for the trek into the tunnel had been short. It was still morning, though the sun was rising steadily overhead. As it did, the day grew hotter. Nathan opened his mouth to answer when they heard a horn honking, and then gunfire and smoke coming from the bank.

Still a distance from the pickup, Nathan squinted up the riverbed in an attempt to see what was going on.

"Rondo!" Ivana scowled.

The drug lord was leaning against José's truck, his own red Chevy pickup parked nearby and populated with men both in back and in the cab. José walked out into the riverbed, still yards away, yet his red face burned with anger. He too, carried a semi-automatic.

"You Gringo!" he called out to them. "I should kill you for stealing my truck. Get away from my sister so I can shoot you." He pointed his gun.

Nathan's hands flew into the air.

"Get lost, José!" Ivana shouted. "I told him to take your damn truck. Where were you? You were supposed to bring us back but you disappeared. You think I want to live at that busted-down cantina?"

"Where do you think these hammers came from, woman? Are you stupid?"

Rondo shot his gun into the air again, his bright smile visible. As they neared, José jumped in his truck.

"Where are you going?" Ivana shouted. The engine revved. Rondo slammed the door of his Chevy. His homies settled in the back, each one carrying a weapon. Rondo backed his truck and spun up over the bank, tires screeching up the hill.

"José! Where are you going?"

"To the dam to raise hell. We've got work to do. We're going to stop the Grays from flooding our tunnels?"

"Wait! Give us a ride!" Ivana panted, running to catch up to him, but he laughed. "I would, sis, but I can't bring him." He nodded toward Nathan. "Rondo says no to the white boy. Too dangerous for you anyway. We'll be putting some holes in some Grays. Catch up if you can or meet me at Papi's!"

"José! Don't." She choked on her scream. She ran, her heart beating to save her brother, but he was gone. "No!"

Two dusty rooster tails chased the path of the trucks as they roared down the road toward the dam.

It was too late. Ivana covered her face. The heat of the day raced into her palms from the fever in her head. Worse than being left alone in the desert, was watching her brother running off to start a fight.

"What if he's killed?" Tears streamed down her face. She knew her brother all too well. Rondo's influence was not a good thing. Add that to his short temper and an explosion brewed. She buried her head in Nathan's shoulder and he hugged her.

"Man, Vana, I don't know. I just don't know. Your dad, Bree, and now José. My mom!" He squeezed her tighter.

His arms were comforting, though nothing could take away the dread of what might happen.

Headwaters

Feeling helpless was the lowest rung in the pit. Unable to give support to someone despondent made things worse. The best Nathan could do was to catch Ivana when she stumbled, although his own footing was equally unstable.

"We'd better get out of the riverbed, Vana. Just in case your brother and his friends don't succeed in stopping the Privatol's mass destruction."

"Friends? They're going to get him killed, Nate. What kind of friend is that?"

Nathan found a trail leading out of the wash and guided Ivana up the hill. She brushed his hand away. "Stop doing that," he said as he grabbed her arm.

"What? I don't need help."

"Well, maybe you don't, but I need to help you." It kept him from breaking down and turning into rubber. If he couldn't help his sister, or Ivana's dad, or even José, he needed to help Ivana. "Please?" His eyes pleaded with her when she glared at him. "Just let me help you."

Thick lashes blinked away a tear. "Okay," she choked out.

The two followed the riverbed from a trail that Nathan presumed was once a shoreline path. Weaving near to sandy valleys and ascending again, sticker bushes pulled at their clothes, and the humid air made them sweat. They had walked for a good portion of the day and just now tips of the cottonwood trees appeared up ahead, and the rumbling sound of the river. Nathan held Ivana back. "What time is it?"

"Two thirty," she answered after pulling her phone from her jeans. "Listen."

More than the sound of the river could be heard. Machine guns.

Nathan ran to the highest hill and from there he saw flashes and heard gunfire. Smoke rose as explosions crackled. Another low roar and a helicopter appeared, firing bullets that ricocheted not far from them.

"Nate, get down!" Ivana yelled. The helicopter turned, diving toward them, its blades singing in the wind. Nathan dodged into the brush as bullets bounced on the dirt around him. Ivana crouched in a crevice between two boulders as the gray M-17 hovered over their hide out.

Nathan held his breath, afraid to move, hoping Ivana would stay still. The enemy circled, lifting higher in to the sky, perhaps the Grays hoped its retreat would draw them out. Not a chance. Eventually the helicopter moved east. It had found its target and fired again, over and over rounds of ammunition flew to the ground. Nathan closed his eyes hoping beyond all hope that it hadn't found José and his gang.

They heard another explosion. The sky lit up with black and red flame and thick blue smoke. Spiraling circles of residue darkened the sky. Nathan slid cautiously next to Ivana and she fell into his arms as they watched the streams of color fold one upon another forming the shape of a dragon's head over their heads. Eyes lit with flame, mouth breathing fire and a voice of thunder clearly speaking. "You found me!"

Ivana's grasp on Nathan's arm tightened at the fearful sight. The final detonation was so loud it shook the Earth, and kept shaking. The trees trembled. Boulders rocked. Both Nathan and Ivana stood.

Ode to the Ant People

The quiet was so ominous that Abree patted her ears to make sure she could still hear, hoping that the ringing was really crickets, like she thought it was. She glanced at each of the other children. Everyone was so hot and tired that speaking would have used up more energy than they could afford. Patty dragged her feet. Makia was well ahead. The other boys walked with their heads low, watching their feet. Makia turned to Abree with his eyes wide.

"Do you smell it?"

"Smell what? My body sweat? Yeah!" Patty complained.

"Water. I smell the river."

Makia was right. There was a distinct odor in the air and Abree could smell it too.

Peter sniffed loudly. "Fish."

"Fish is good."

They were too spent to cheer, but the mood changed and they stepped quicker. Even the temperature dropped a degree or two.

"We are very near the dam. Listen!" Makia stopped them again and they heard a rumble.

"Shouldn't we climb out of the river bed soon?" Abree asked eyeing the steep bank around them. "It's really steep here but maybe we'll come across a way out up ahead. If we do we should take advantageous of it."

"It looks like there's an easy trail out by those old cattails just beyond that ironwood tree. Come on!"

The children broke into a run, but stopped suddenly when an

explosion rumbled the earth.

"What's that?"

Another explosion, and then a rushing sound, like water. A flow of mud trickled in the riverbed, inching toward their feet. Makai was the first to come out of shock. "Flood! Quick!" He ran toward the stand of cattails with Abree and the others close at his heels.

Reunion

A stream of muddy water trickled into the basin below them. Nathan pulled Ivana further up the bank as the entire landscape burst into spray and dust and smoke. A wall of water shot into the sky, crashing down with such magnitude the trees trembled at the sound.

Nathan and Ivana grappled over the bank, climbing a step higher and watched the water fill the riverbed almost instantly. Fingers of wet grabbed at every shallow, every ravine and every nook that lay waiting for it. Muddy waters thick and foaming spilled over the edges of its channel racing forward, ecstatic over its freedom. The spray reached their faces. The water tasted sweet, the air refreshing.

The site mesmerized them as the river rumbled in rage. Magnificent in its power it swallowed up everything in its path, bubbling and churning with unrestrained energy. The wall of water raged into the old riverbed for miles south.

The dam had burst.

There was nowhere else to go now. Nathan and Ivana watched from the road and when the river settled into its home again, they walked down to the shore. The dust, smoke, and trauma settled into the dying day as the sun set, the river reflecting twilight's pinks and gold.

For Nathan, it was healing to watch the water, the current finally settled, the shallows snatching bits of debris that the flood had stolen. Nathan stood among the reeds and reached for an object floating below the surface. When he pulled it out. His heart stopped.

"Ivana!" He would have cried, but he was too stunned. In his hands, muddy and torn by the raging river, was his Harley bandana, the one he had given Abree.

Ivana came to his side, her expression as pale as his. "There are a lot of Harley bandanas in this world, you know"

He wrung the water from the cloth, squeezing it with his fist.

"Nathan…."

He barely heard her —panic racing too hard within. "No!"

"It's just the bandana, Nate. It doesn't mean she drowned. It just means she's not in the tunnel, and she's not in prison. If it's hers, that is."

Nathan crumbled to the ground and buried his head in his knees. There was nothing Ivana could do to move him. He would stay there and mourn.

Time passed until the moon peeked out over the trees. When he woke—or came to—from where he had been, he looked up and found Ivana sitting next to him.

"Why are you still here?" he asked.

"What was I going to do? Go find my dead brother? Go count how many holes they nailed him with? Or maybe he's just ashes." She'd been crying. Her eyes were red, her hair matted.

"You don't know that he's dead."

She snickered. "Right. Neither do you know that Abree is, but there's a lot more chance of my brother having been shot up than your sister drowned."

What could he say? Only the sound of rushing water, crickets, and frogs could ease their troubled minds, so he let the songs of the night take over.

After a quiet moment, Ivana spoke. "It was Quetzalcoatl that we saw."

"I know it."

"He looked just like he did in my dreams. To think he was up there in the sky like that."

"What is it that he said? I wasn't sure I heard him right."

"He said, 'You have found them'."

"Whom was he talking about?"

"The ant people, dummy. That's who he's been talking about all along."

A breeze rustled the reeds in the waters below. A bullfrog croaked.

"Who are the ant people?" Nathan asked.

"I don't know, Nate. Maybe they're like the little guys. You know, the ones that mind their own business. Stay out of politics." She broke a blade of grass and chewed on the end. "The ones who always find something nice to say about people and never cause trouble." She wiped her eyes.

Nathan gazed at the moon rays dancing on the water. "Quetzalcoatl says we found them?"

"That's what he says."

The waters stirred where the reeds grew. It could have been a frog jumping from a lily pad, but then the river stirred again. It was no frog. "Shh, Vana. There's something in the water. Look."

"Probably some big old catfish got caught in a pool after the flood."

"Maybe, but maybe not. Quiet."

His eyes were fixed on the shallow beach just around the corner from the ironwood tree they sat under. Stiff reeds that had dried the year before still stood rooted near shore, and something was moving under them.

"My God, Nate. What is it?"

Mud bubbled as the reeds lifted out of the shallows. Figures emerged from under them, slimy and mud laden. One figure sat up, and then another. Coughing and sputtering, they shook their heads violently, ridding the mud from their faces.

"People!" Ivana gasped.

"Children." Nathan whispered.

Pulling the reeds from their mouths, one of them laughed, and the others joined in. They spat and wiped the thick substance from their cheeks, their eyes, and their noses. Unaware that anyone was watching them, the children pulled their bodies from the sucking slime and waded carefully into the river, ducking their heads under the water, splashing themselves clean, and splashing each other. They played in the rays of the moon as its light sparkled on the ripples that they made.

Ivana stepped up to Nathan, the two still concealed in the shadows.

She whispered in his ear. "Look at that girl over there, Nate. She looks like your sister."

Nathan's hand fidgeted with the bandana inside his pocket. What if it were Abree? He couldn't tell. It was so dark, and this girl was older than he remembered his sister to be. He stepped forward away from the trees, onto the beach, and into the moonlight.

"Abree?" he called. Not loud. He didn't want to startle any of the children, but they stopped when he spoke.

The girl turned, standing knee deep in the water. She looked at him, her dark silhouette backlit by the stars.

"Abree? It's me. Nathan."

She didn't answer.

A dark-haired boy leaned toward her. "Do you know that man, Abree?"

The girl walked toward shore. Nathan met her where the river tickled their toes. They took a moment to check each other's faces. He had to be certain it was she, though now he knew it was.

She smiled.

He tried to speak, but there were no words fitting.

She jumped into his arms and he swung her around, kissing her hair, lifting her into the sky. She giggled. He laughed. They cried and then they held each other as if never to let go.

Planting Stick

"Children on the farm again. Oh, Ivana dear, you don't know how this blesses my heart!" Auntie Flora had already filled the muffin tins twice. This third time she found some raisins to put in the dough and handed the bowl and spoon to Patty. "She's one of my favorites already. Love the red top." She gave Patty a squeeze and patted her head. The girl was a good few inches taller than Aunt Flora.

"It's good to have a home again Auntie," Patty said, grinning at Nathan who stood by the screen door.

"When the good Lord takes something away, he brings it back in plenty!" Auntie Flora always gave credit to her God. Nathan could appreciate that. This family had been through more than any he'd known, but maybe things would be better now. How could it not with all these happy children helping Auntie Flora in the kitchen?

Ivana stood on the porch in blue jeans and rubber boots, and a spade in her hand. "Ready?"

Nathan nodded. There was planting to do and it would take all day and some of the next. "Where is Jerry?"

"He's with Papi at José's grave. They're talking."

José had been buried on the farm the night of the shootout. Jerry had left the cantina and walked almost to the dam that night. He heard the shooting, and saw the Quetzalcoatl in the sky, just like Nathan and Ivana had. When he didn't see Rondo's truck return, he figured the worse had happened. Jerry thought to bring the body back; sneaking him in the dark after the Grays had left. He carried José all the way to Papi's farm, the limp body thrown over his shoulder like a sack of potatoes. That was a week ago.

"It's going to be sad for everyone for a while," Nathan said.

"Still, without the tunnels, the Grays won't be so concerned about us anymore. Not for a while."

He looked at her. "What about Rondo? What about the guys that were protecting your farm?"

"What? You think he's the only drug lord around here?" she snickered. "Get real, Nate! He's got family. No Cartel bury their dead alone. Always they find the responsible ones and toss their corpses in a mass grave as tribute. You can bet on it."

Ivana slapped Nathan gently on his back. "As for us, Garcias are strong. What's important now is we have a life again. Look at Auntie. Don't you love seeing her happy?"

Nathan watched the woman cooking with the children, giving each of them either a job to do or a spoon to lick. Abree caught his gaze and smiled, her nose curled up and her eyes twinkled. With hands buried in masa, Abree was content. Makia diced onions and winked at Nathan.

"Let's go, Nate. There's work to do." Ivana tugged on his arm.

Nathan nodded. "I guess we can look forward to getting the crops that we plant. I can't return to the US now. It's too overwhelming."

"No one ever asked you to go back, man."

"But there are people yet to save, Ivana." He thought mostly of Ivana's father.

"Who do you think you are? Superman?"

"It'd be nice if I were."

"Well, you're not. Stop pouting about it. None of us are super powered. We did what we could for now."

Nathan nodded as he stepped outside and gazed out at the barren field, tilled and ready. The morning sun coated the sky with gold.

"For now," she repeated. ""Maybe we didn't save the world, yet, Nate. Still, we did save some good seed, and some children." Ivana hooked her arm into his as they walked out to the cornfield. "That's really all it takes to make a new world, isn't it?"

Acknowledgments

Many thanks to the people who made this story possible including my critique partners, my concept editor Gwen Perkins, my first publisher Kim Mutch Emerson and MKSP who put out the first edition.

I've since gone over the story and rewrote some of the lumpy spots. I hope you enjoy this adventure as much as I enjoyed writing it!

And to my readers—

Thank you for reading Altered! I hope you enjoyed this book. If you have a comment, please feel free to leave a review.

If you'd like to know a little more about me, here's where you can start, and then please do visit my website to see some of my artwork and my other books
http://gardnersart.com

I live in the Pacific Northwest. After living in the dry desert of Arizona for over 23 years, I tired of always praying for rain, so I decided to come and get it on my own. Gray skies and deep forests give way to the most glorious summers you could ever imagine. Not to mention the abundance of berries, clams, oysters, salmon, fruits of all kinds, to me the Puget Sound area of Washington is the richest place in the world. I have seven children, all grown. Sixteen grandchildren that need stories written, and so they are my inspiration.

People always find it fascinating that I lived in a mud house for over 13 years, hauling water from the well in a bucket, cooking on a wood stove, planting blue corn in desert washes, and generally living out of the box. Some of these experiences are written into my novels.

If you enjoyed this book, please leave a review.
You can see my complete portfolio of books and film on my website.
http://gardnersart.com

Motif from *Ancient Mexico Motif*

www.ingramcontent.com/pod-product-compliance
Lightning Source LLC
Chambersburg PA
CBHW020908180626
46816CB00007BA/2296